Retribution
By Mohammad Al Onaizi

Preface

I embarked on my journey to write my first novel around 4 years ago. I love writing; I have written many poems, and have also worked as a blogger and copywriter on two separate occasions. I am not an extrovert and therefore see writing as the best way to express myself. I had the idea for this story and I pitched it to my elder brother who had recently succeeded in selling a script for a television series. He didn't like my idea, but that didn't stop me and I decided to write it myself instead. The only idea I had to begin with, was a rich man killing a poor man. I felt that it was an intriguing concept to begin with, as people would want to know why that happened. I liked the sense of mystery and suspense which accompanied that simple idea. I first started by just writing that idea down and slowly, more ideas came to me as to how the story would shape up. The main characters of the story are Larry Stone, David Lawrence, Sarah Phillips and Jason Kay. It just started with Larry and David, the rich man and poor man. But as more ideas came to me, I decided to add Sarah and Jason as key characters in the story. I even tried to insert a bit of my personality while building the character of Larry Stone, the protagonist of the story. The rest of the characters are not based on any real-life individuals and are purely fictional. I would classify my book as fiction; although I researched the legal issues that were addressed in the story to see if I was accurate, I still made sure that the story would continue on the path I intended it to, even if it meant that some legal scenes in the story would be factually inaccurate. The story starts with the aforementioned idea of a rich man killing a poor man, and then, it goes back in time to see how these two characters met each other in the first place. Along the way, the story will go back and forth in time, so I hope nobody gets lost while reading it. Writing this novel has been one of the most enjoyable things I have ever done in my life, so enjoyable in fact, that I am in the process of finishing up my second novel, a prequel to this, which will include the culmination of three of the previously mentioned characters. But first, I hope you enjoy this suspense filled drama, which has everything from greed and betrayal, to a character that everyone in this story feared, a character who's story will be told in the second part to this novel.

Dedication
This book is dedicated to everyone who helped and
encouraged me to write it.

PROLOGUE

(News headline)

Millionaire Larry Stone Arrested For First-Degree Murder, Trial To Begin Next Week.

(News coverage, two journalists discussing)

Larry Stone, as we all know, is a well-established man and has come a long way into building what is now an empire. David Lawrence, on the other hand, was a nobody. He was in his 40's, unemployed, and divorced. So the question on everyone's mind is why? Why would Larry Stone risk everything he has worked for to kill a common man like David Lawrence??

(Reporter outside courtroom)

Everyone is anticipating hearing what's written in Mr Lawrence's will, because according to his lawyer, David Lawrence's will is the key to this whole case, and it will answer all of our questions, and will finally put this case, which has rocked the country, to bed.

10 Years Ago

PART ONE

BEGINNING

1

Jack Stone is a hardworking family man, who is married to Lindsey Stone, a nurse at the local hospital. They have a 17 year old son named Larry, who would always try to copy Jack and wants to follow in his footsteps. Jack's love for business led him to work for a successful company in Michigan. After his father returned from work, Larry would look at the paperwork that Jack would have with him, in order to understand what business was all about.

"How do you understand all of this? It looks confusing" Larry asked his dad.

"Heh, you will get used to it" his dad replied.

"Yeah, I think I will stay away from all of this now. I will wait till I finish college" Larry said.

Lindsey was reading the paper when she came across a story that caught her eye.

"Isn't that your boss?" Lindsey asked Jack.

"Let me see…yeah, that's him" Jack replied.

'Local Businessman Loses Fortune After Investment Gamble'.

"Did anybody mention this at work today?" Lindsey asked.

"No, this is the first time I have heard about it. Wow, he lost a lot of money. This could be bad for us. There may be a mass firing this week", Jack said.

"Do you think you might get fired also?" asked Lindsey.

"…I'm not really sure what goes on in his mind. But I have a pretty important role in his company so I don't think he will fire me. Fingers crossed!" Jack exclaimed cautiously.

Lindsey's concern, however, was on point, because when Jack went to work the next day he learnt that an entire department had been shut down, with 12 employees receiving their pink slips. Jack was one of them.

"I'm so sorry honey", Lindsey tried to console her husband.

"That's not fair dad, you work so hard for that guy and then he fires you", Larry was angered.

"Life's not fair, what are you gonna do about it?" Jack replied.

"What are you gonna do now?" Lindsey asked.

"He actually recommended me to the owner of another company", said Jack.

"That's good, so you are gonna take that job offer?" Lindsey asked.

"…I don't know, we'll see", Jack replied.

Jack didn't want to take a job where there was no sense of job security. He had just lost his job because of a mistake his boss had made. And all his hard work for that company was for nothing. He did not want to face that same situation again. He waited until after they finished dinner and only when he was alone with Lindsey, did he tell her what he planned to do with his career now.

"I wanna start my own business! I hate that I'm not my own boss and that I can be fired at anytime", Jack explained.

"That's not a bad idea, but what business can you start here?" asked Lindsey.

"No, not here. I was thinking of New York", Jack said.

"You want us to move?" Lindsey asked.

"Why not? Every hospital needs nurses, I'm sure if you apply, that a hospital will not turn you down." Jack said.

"I'm more worried about you honey, are you sure this is what you want?" Lindsey asked him.

"Yes, I have enough money saved for me to start a small business. This is what I want", answered Jack.

"What about Larry? Do you think he will be okay with the decision to move?" Lindsey asked.

"I think he will be okay with it. This might be a good thing for him. I worry that he spends too much time with us, he doesn't have any friends. This might be a new start for him, to make some friends and socialize", Jack said.

"Alright then, I guess we are moving to New York!" Lindsey was excited about the move. The next day, they informed Larry and he was also excited to move although he was still upset about his dad's firing.

"I can't believe how you're letting him get away with this though. You didn't deserve to get fired", Larry told his dad.

"Yeah but he has a lot of connections, if I try to fight him then he will make sure I won't get a job anywhere. Sometimes, it's best just to forget about it and move on", explained Jack.

Jack and Lindsey travelled to New York for the weekend to look for a new home. They found a perfect place just outside the city. They convinced the realtor to let them pay the first instalment now, and they would pay the rest once they sell their current home in Michigan. It didn't take long for them to find a buyer for their home. Once the deal had gone through, they went back to New York and paid the full amount for their new home. And when Larry finished his last year of high school, the family was ready for the big move to New York. Jack hoped that this move would be the start of a new chapter in his professional career. Little did he know, it would turnout to be the last chapter of his life.

Larry always looked up to his dad and wanted to be like him. Even though Larry didn't have the knack for business, his dad still encouraged him to keep working hard. Larry wasn't sociable and he considered his parents to be his friends also. Larry was hit pretty hard when his dad was fired from his job and after he graduated high school, Larry decided to forgo college and instead, help his dad set up a small business. It took the family a couple of months before they finally settled into their new home.

PART TWO
JUST A CLOSE FRIENDSHIP

2

David Lawrence was a successful stock broker from New York. He was married and has one daughter. He was the kind of person who shied away from the spotlight and preferred to be the guy in the background who does all the dirty work, and he was happy with that because he was managing to make a nice living for himself and his family. David loved his job, not just because of the good money that he made, but because he managed to gain something that few people manage to get from work; he had formed a close friendship with his boss and his colleagues. The only problem that he could never solve was getting his wife, Jennifer, to join his group when they hung out on the weekends. David and his colleagues would always reward themselves with an office party every time they successfully brought in a large amount of money to the company. David finally convinced his wife to come to the latest party that they were having, where he also introduced her to his closest colleague.

"Honey, this is Sarah Phillips. Sarah, this is my wife Jennifer", David introduced them to each other.

"It's nice to meet you, Sarah, David has told me so much about you, he says that you are the real genius of the company", said Jennifer.

"You actually said that about me?" Sarah laughed. "If our company has a genius, it is definitely David. I just look at him while he is working and I'm just amazed, he's like a magician. We are all begging him to start his own thing because he would make a lot of money if he was leading a company. I'm telling you, if I were you, I would hold on to this man because he is going to be a millionaire one day, I'm sure of it!" Sarah jokingly responded.

Jennifer didn't quite appreciate Sarah's joke. She also felt that there may be more than a friendship between the two, and after Sarah left, she confronted David about this issue.

"Honey, not this again. That was the reason I wanted to introduce you to her, so that you could see we are just friends. There is nothing to worry about", David explained.

"I just got a bad vibe from her, I didn't like her", Jennifer responded.

"Fine, I will just finish my beer and then we will leave", said David.

David was not that much of a drinker. Being in his 30's, it was hard for him to keep up with his 20 something year old colleagues drinking habits. That one beer was his usual limit. David introduced his wife to the rest of his co-workers, they chatted a bit, he finished his beer and then they went back home. Needless to say, Jennifer did not enjoy the office party. And she definitely didn't like Sarah. To Jennifer's bad luck, the next day when she was out with her daughter, she ran into Sarah at the mall. She didn't want to say hello to her, but she was thinking about David and how he might be upset if she ignored his colleague and friend.

"…Sarah, hi. How are you?" Jennifer asked.

"…Oh hi, Jennifer right? I'm good, how are you?" Sarah didn't recall her name at first, which upset Jennifer a bit.

"I'm good," Jennifer replied.

"And who is this little cutie?" Sarah said as she bent down to shake hands with Jennifer's daughter.

"This is Bonnie, our daughter", replied Jennifer.

"Oh, she's so cute. David told me he had a daughter, it's the first time I am seeing her. Hi Bonnie", Sarah said.

"Hi", Bonnie replied.

"She looks just like her dad", Sarah said.

"So…we've got a busy day ahead of us. We have to get going. It was nice running into you", Jennifer just wanted this encounter to end.

"It was nice seeing you, too. Say hi to Dave for me", Sarah said.

David was not with Jennifer because he was out with two of his other colleagues, Frank Akerman and Jason Kay. They were meeting up at a cafe, and David was already there waiting for his friends to show up.

"Hey Dave, you're here early", Frank said in surprise as he arrived on time at the restaurant to see David already at the table.

"You know I don't like to make people wait for me, I always come early. Unfortunately, the same can't be said about the one who has yet to arrive", David joked.

"It's Jason, what do you expect?" Frank laughed.

The two of them chatted for half an hour before Jason finally arrived.

"Hey guys, you're here early", Jason said

"No we're here on time, you are late", David corrected him.

"...Yeah, I was hoping you wouldn't notice, sorry about that...so what were you guys talking about?" Jason asked.

"I was trying to convince him about starting his own thing, again", Frank answered.

"Yes! Dude, please. I wanna come work for you. I'm getting tired of our boss." Jason said.

"What? But you're so friendly with him, always joking and laughing", David said.

"I'm just acting. You see me laughing and joking with him, but what I really wanna do is just choke him! He's so annoying", Jason complained.

"Do you see David? Do you see what you're doing to poor Jason her?" Frank joked.

"...Help me." Jason said to David, with a sad look on his face.

"But seriously Dave, what is holding you back? Is it the money?" Frank asked him.

"No I have enough money to start something", David replied.

"So you have money, and you also have people who are willing to come work for you", Frank told him.

"Yes, I agree with that. If you start a business I'm sure everyone at work will choose to work for you, even if you offer a lower salary", Jason said.

"Really?" David asked.

"I talk to everyone in our company and I can tell you that you are held in high regard by all of them. They all like you, and I agree with Jason that they would jump at the chance to work for you", Frank said, "Do you hate being in charge that much?"

"It's not that I hate it, it's just that I don't like the extra responsibilities that come with being in charge. I mean, can you see me yelling at somebody or firing them when they do something wrong? I'm just happy with the way I am now, I go in and out of work without anyone noticing me", David explained.

"I see your point, so I have got an idea for you - put me in charge", Jason told David, "It will be your company, you do all the work the way you want, but on paper, it will be my company. Whenever there are any duties that the person in charge has to deal with, I will deal with them. You trust me don't you?" Jason asked David.

"Trust is a funny word", David replied.

"Seriously Dave, that's not a bad idea. It will be exactly how you are now, you can do all the work that you want and nobody will bother you because everybody will think that Jason is in charge. All the press related issues, the employees - it will all be on Jason", Frank said.

"Yes! But you have to call me sir or master in front of everyone so that they believe I'm in charge", Jason joked.

"Just ignore the last part. What do you say?" Frank asked David.

"Ok, I will think about it", David finally gave into his colleagues' demands, and had seriously begun thinking of leaving the company and starting his own.

Even though David was now thinking about starting his own company, it didn't deter him from his work for his current company, and in the following month, the company, behind David's ingenuity, brought in an even larger amount of money. That, of course, called for an even bigger office party. They scheduled a date for the party, which would be held as usual at Jason's beach house. But David's colleagues were planning a surprise for him, and they managed to keep the surprise a secret until the day of the party, which would turn out to be a night full of surprises.

PART THREE

LARRY'S STRUGGLES

3

"Damn it! I can't believe I got it wrong again, I'm such a screw-up!" Larry was still finding it hard to help establish his dad's business. His dad would always give him a short quiz to test his knowledge, but Larry would always fail at his dad's quizzes.

"Hey, you are not a screw-up", Jack tried to console him. "Do you think I knew anything about business at your age? You will make mistakes, you just gotta learn from them."

"Yeah, okay. Hey mom, what's for dinner?" Larry turned towards his mother.

"Spaghetti with meatballs", Lindsey replied, "It's your turn to cook next weekend."

"Yeah I know", Larry said.

"Have you figured out what you are going to make? I really liked the Mac and Cheese that you made last time", His mom said.

"I'm thinking of doing something else. It's a surprise", Larry smiled.

"A surprise or you still have no idea?" His dad joked.

"A surprise!" Larry replied.

"By the way, dad, are we gonna go shooting tomorrow?" Larry and his dad loved to go shoot at the shooting range. Jack even had his own gun, a Desert Eagle.

"Yeah sure, we can go shooting tomorrow." His dad replied.

Larry wanted to go shooting so that he could clear his mind. They made their way to the shooting range where Jack's friend, Steve Nichols, was already waiting for them.

"You guys are late. We shot all the targets already", Steve said to them.

"Even if all the targets were here, Larry would still miss all of them", Jack said, making fun of his son.

Larry shoved Jack playfully. "Hey, I shot more targets than you last time. We gotta keep score this time. I will beat you both today, you will see", he said.

Larry was very competitive and he always wanted to win at everything that he did. But the competitiveness and fight in his heart were never matched by his abilities. He lost the mini competition with his dad and Steve.

"Are you sure he's your son Jack? He's nowhere near as good a shooter as you. C'mon Larry! You gotta practice more", Steve said to him.

"If you manage to shoot all the targets next time, my gun will be your 18th birthday present ", Jack challenged him.

"Alright, I will keep practicing", Larry replied to Steve. Then turning towards his father, he said, "I accept your challenge too dad, I will take that gun from you!" Larry then left to go to the bathroom.

"Hey, how's Lindsey? Did you guys find out the sex of the baby?" Steve asked Jack.

"She's doing well. Yeah we went to the doctor the other day, Larry here is gonna have a little sister", Jack responded.

"Congratulations! She must have been very happy to hear that!" Steve exclaimed.

Jack chuckled. "Oh, she acted like a little child. She was clapping her hands shouting "I'm gonna have a girl, I'm gonna have a girl!" Even the doctors couldn't help but laugh. It made me really happy to see how happy she was because the miscarriage hit her really hard. But she always wanted a girl, so we went to the doctor's to see if it was safe for her to get pregnant again. She was feeling good and the doctor gave us the green light, and here we are a couple of months later and she is pregnant with a girl. I just hope things go well this time", he said.

"Man that's great, I'm really happy for you guys. How did Larry take the news? Was he happy?" Steve asked.

"I hope he is, I don't really know what his happy face looks like."

"So the therapist isn't helping?"

"He went to her a couple of times but I think he needs to figure out what's bothering him on his own."

"He's a good kid, hope he gets out of whatever it is he's going through. You know, if Mark was his age I would have introduced him to Larry, that way he can have someone to hang out with." Steve was talking about his oldest son, Mark.

"Ha, really? A 35 year-old retired Marine and a 17 year-old loner becoming friends? That's some movie." Jack sarcastically responded.

"Call me crazy, but I see some Mark in Larry", Steve said

Jack faces the targets, raises his arms and shoots. He fires five shots which hit the middle of the target and he turns around to face Steve. "You're crazy!"

Larry decided to spend even more time at the office to try and understand more about the business. He also utilized his time to study from the many books that he had bought. His dad, however, didn't like what Larry was doing because he thought he would eventually burn out from working too hard. Jack decided to arrange a night out for the family, mainly to get Larry away from work and spend some family time, and he called Larry to tell him about it.

"C'mon son, you are killing yourself with the extra work. Look, the business is set, you can relax a little. Don't worry too much", Jack told him.

"I know the business is set now, but I don't feel that I'm helping enough. To be honest with you dad, I still don't know what I'm doing. I want to prove to you and more importantly to myself that I'm cut out to be in the business world. So I'm going to respectfully decline your invitation to dinner. Now it's just a romantic date with you and mom", Larry continued with a chuckle, "I'm just gonna finish the book that I'm on now, close up the office and come home. You and mom go enjoy yourselves and I will see you guys when you come back home."

"Well, you are talking like a businessman! Alright son, do as you wish. But remember one thing, you have nothing to prove to me! I'm already proud of the fact that you want to follow my footsteps. You are right. You might not know what you are doing now. But that's okay, you are still young. You will grow and learn, and one day, this business will become yours and I'm sure when that time comes, you will know what to do. Just don't stress yourself too much now, alright? Love you son", Jack said, beaming with pride.

"Alright dad, love you too", replied Larry.

Jack's words couldn't have been more poignant, as that would be the last conversation he had with his son.

David Lawrence was dressed, ready to go to that scheduled work party at Jason's beach house. Jennifer declined to go with him this time, and she decided to make plans with her friends.

"Is Sarah going to be there?" Jennifer asked.

"Of course she is gonna be there she works with me. Look, I'm really getting tired of this, I understand if you don't trust her but you gotta at least trust me."

"You're right, I'm sorry." Jennifer apologized.

"You sure you don't wanna come?" He asked.

"Yeah, I don't wanna hear another millionaire reference."

"It was a joke!"

"I don't think it was, I think it shows what is more important to her. Anyway, have fun honey."

Jennifer hugged him goodbye as he left the apartment. But as he did, his phone beeped. He looked at his phone to see a message from Sarah saying that her ride for the party cancelled, and she needed a lift. David replied to her that he can pick her up, but he decided not to share this information with his wife, since he could obviously see she was jealous of Sarah. David made his way to pick Sarah up, and they arrived at Jason's beach house where he was surprised to see a banner with his name on it hanging on the wall. Since he was the brains behind the company's latest achievement, the group decided to have this party in his honor.

David was out at the party, Jack and Lindsey were out on their date, and Larry was still at the office. But he was getting both tired and sleepy, so he decided to call it a night, and close up at the office and head back home. He took the bus back home and when he arrived, it was very late at night and he had expected to find his parents home, but he noticed that the car was not in the driveway. He checked his phone to see if maybe he missed any messages from his parents saying that they might be late, but there was no such message. He called his dad but there was no answer. Larry didn't worry so much since he just figured that it was the weekend and it had been a long time since his parents had been out on a date, so maybe they were enjoying their night out. Larry ate his dinner and went to sleep, expecting to wake up the next morning to have breakfast with his parents. Instead, he was woken up by a phone call at 4 in the morning. He groggily got out of bed, and went down to the living room to pick the phone up. The speaker was set on the kitchen counter, and the phone had been ringing for what seemed like an hour, but he finally reached the phone and picked it up.

"Hello, is this Mr. Larry Stone?" The female caller asked.

"Yes..." Larry answered.

"I'm Nurse Henderson from the University Medical Hospital. I am sorry to inform you that your parents were in a car accident last night. Could you please come to the hospital?"

"WHAT?? ARE THEY OK??" Larry anxiously asked.

"It would be better if you could come to the hospital." The nurse was obviously hesitant in sharing more information with Larry.

"NO! TELL ME NOW! ARE THEY OK?" Larry yelled into the phone.

"I'm afraid...they passed away...I'm sorry." The nurse had no choice but to break the news to him over the phone. When she did, all she could hear from Larry's end was silence.

"Hello? Sir we would like you to come to the hospital to identify the bodies." The nurse said.

Larry just collapsed on the floor and began to cry uncontrollably. At that moment, he had so many thoughts rushing through his head. The day that Jack said Larry would take over the company, has come sooner than he had wanted.

'How am I gonna take care of myself? What am I gonna do now? Where do I even begin? What about the business? I can't do this on my own? THIS CAN'T BE HAPPENING!!' He thought to himself.

Larry has been lying on the floor now for an hour. He had stopped crying and thinking. His world had become silent and all that was audible was the beeping phone that he had never closed. He managed to pick himself up and take a cab to the hospital to go see his perished parents.

"I'm Larry Stone, the hospital called me to identify my parent's bodies." The shocked nurse, who was different from the one that called him, didn't expect him to be so young.

"Is there nobody else who can identify the bodies? Maybe an uncle or a family friend?" The nurse was overwhelmed by the look of sadness on Larry's young face and didn't want him to see his dead parents.

"No, it's just me. Don't prolong this thing with stupid questions! I just want to identify the bodies and get it over with and go home", Larry said.

The nurse led him to the morgue where he saw all the different dead bodies, set on metal slabs, covered in white sheet. They went over to two bodies that were placed next to each other, and she slowly uncovered the sheet to show their faces. Larry surprisingly, did not shed any tears, as he looked at his parents lying dead. He took a few seconds just staring at their faces, hoping that they were going to open their eyes, but that was something that they were never going to do again.

"It's them", was his only response, and he said it while showing no emotion on his face.

For the next two weeks, Larry would shut himself out from the outside world. The short staff employees at his dad's company were calling him but he wasn't answering, and they had to make do without their deceased boss or his son. The only person he talked to was Steve, who invited him over to his security company in hopes of luring him to work for him. But finally, a time came when he wanted to get out of the house, since staying at home had begun suffocating him. He went out to have a walk and clear his head. It was late at night, and as he was walking with his hands in his pockets and his head up looking at the stars, his mind wandered. He was not paying attention to where he was going, and unintentionally, bumped into two guys.

"Hey, watch where you're going dumbass," one of the guys said.

"Sorry", Larry apologized.

"Who the hell walks without looking where they are going?" the guy said.

"He was looking at the stars. Do you want to phone home?" The other guy joked.

"I said I was sorry", Larry apologized again.

Larry didn't want any trouble and decided to just walk away from them.

"Hey, where are you going?" One of them said. They didn't want to fight Larry because he was much younger than them and clearly not physically up to par with them. They just wanted to tease him a little more.

"It's probably time for him to go to bed so his mommy can read him a bedtime story", the other guy said.

Larry just stopped in his tracks at the mention of his mother. As he had his back turned to them, he could hear them laughing. Larry was now clinching his fists. He had never gotten in a fight his whole life, but his emotions got the better of him and he just turned around knocked down one guy and jumped on the other. However, he was quickly overpowered by the two men who proceeded to deliver a beating to Larry. He was on the ground with his arms up trying to protect himself from the punches and kicks that were coming his way. The men only stopped when they heard the approaching sound of police sirens. But they weren't able to run away, and all three men were arrested and taken to the police station. Larry was sitting on a bench in the police station. He was handcuffed, with a bloodied and bruised face, and a bewildered look on his face. He was looking around at all the police officers, and the criminals they were bringing in, and it was all an alien scene for him. An officer approached to tell him that he can make one call, but Larry didn't know whom to call, and thought his only hope was Steve Nichols.

"Hello", Judy, Steve's wife answered instead.

"Hello, it's Larry Stone", Larry said.

"Larry, how are you doing honey?" Judy inquired.

"I'm in the police station. I got in a fight and I don't know what to do, can Steve come to help me?" Larry went straight to the point.

"Oh sweetie, what happened? That's not like you. Steve isn't here, but Mark is. I will tell him to come to you right away. Did you contact your lawyer?" Judy asked.

"No, I don't have a lawyer", Larry said.

"I will call your parent's lawyer, Mr. Beigler. I have his number, I will tell him to go meet you as well", Judy said.

"Thank you", Larry said.

Larry ended his call and he was escorted back to the bench he was sitting on. It wasn't long after he hung up the phone that he saw the intimidating figure of Mark, Steve's eldest son walking into the police station. He was followed by Paul Beigler, his parent's lawyer. As Beigler went to complete the procedure to release Larry, Mark came over to Larry.

"Are you okay?" Mark asked.

"I think my nose is broken", Larry replied.

"Is that them?" Mark asked as he pointed to two guys who were sitting on the bench opposite Larry, and were still staring at him.

"Yeah, that's them", Larry said.

"I will take care of them. You tell your lawyer to drop you back home", Mark said as he stared back at the two guys. Both of them looked away quickly. One could tell from Mark's look that he was not the kind of guy anyone would want to mess with. His toned arms looked as though they were sculpted, and his face, with the five o'clock shadow, showed the wear and tear of a man that had been in wars since the day he was born. He stayed back after Paul finished and took Larry home. No police officer even tried to approach Mark, as he made himself comfortable on the bench. While Larry was bewildered, Mark was right at home amid all the commotion that was going on around him. Mark was waiting for the two guys to leave as well, and when they did, he got up and followed them out of the police station without them noticing that he was on their tail. He kept to the shadows and followed them until they had gone a clear distance of the police station, before confronting them.

"Pick on someone your own size", Mark said to them.

Unlike Larry, Mark had been in many fights and he was able to defend himself better, and when he was done, the two men were laying motionless on the ground, without a single scratch on him. He then calmly walked away, and went back home.

The next day, Larry decided that it was best to stay home, and nurse his bandaged broken nose. He was sitting alone, staring at the muted television. He was waiting to smell the aroma coming from the kitchen -an indication that his mom was preparing dinner, or to see the front door open and watch his dad walk in with his briefcase after a long day's work. It was finally sinking in that he will never experience those little moments ever again, and that thought made him very uneasy. He went up to his parents' bedroom and opened the locked jewellery box where his dad would keep his Desert Eagle. He took it out and loaded just one bullet and pointed the gun at his temple. He was going to kill himself, not because he had lost his parents, but because he blamed himself for their death, because he regretted not going with them that night; he wanted to die with them. He remained there with the gun pointed at his temple for a few minutes, and he still hadn't pulled the trigger. Strangely enough, not many thoughts were going through his head at that point. His mind was blank, and he was holding the gun but he wasn't thinking about pulling the trigger, it was as if he was waiting for the gun to fire by itself. The front door bell rang which made Larry jump and quickly put the gun back in the box. He went down to see who it was. It was Steve and Judy, they had come over to visit Larry and see how he was doing.

"Hey Larry, how are you son?" Steve asked Larry as Judy gave him a hug.

"I don't know, I'm still sad, confused…I'm not sure what to do now." Larry said, as Judy wiped a tear from his eye.

"Why don't you come stay with us for a while, we have plenty of room. You shouldn't stay here all by yourself", Judy said to Larry.

"Thanks, but I think I'm gonna stay here", Larry replied politely.

"Remember Larry, we are here for you. Anytime you need anything - don't hesitate to tell us. You have our phone number and you know where we live, drop by anytime. Here, take this for now. If you ever need more money let me know", Steve gave Larry an envelope with money.

"Thank you", Larry said.

"Steve, why don't you offer him a job at the company? You went over to see it the other day didn't you?" Judy asked Larry, referring to Steve's security company.

"No, I don't want to. I want to complete what my dad started building, I want to make him proud…" Larry said.

"I understand son, but a position for you is always available if you ever change your mind and want to come work for me", Steve said, "By the way, Mark was asking about you. He wanted us to give you his number. You should give him a call sometime."

It seemed as though Steve and Judy unknowingly saved Larry's life by visiting him. But that wasn't the case, because even if they hadn't come, Larry still wouldn't have pulled the trigger and ended his life. But their visit did help Larry feel that he wasn't entirely alone, that there were still people who loved him and cared about him. Larry took Mark's number not knowing what he wanted from him. He met him when he visited Steve's security company, and again at the police station. He was scared to call Mark because the two times he had met him, he had been intimidated by him. But then, he thought he should call to at least thank him for coming to the police station to help him. He went to sit on the couch with the piece of paper with Mark's number in one hand, and the telephone speaker in the other.

"…Um…hello?" Larry stammered.

"Larry?" Mark asked.

"Yes…your parents gave me your phone number. I just wanted to call to thank you for helping me out", Larry said.

"Meet me in the park in half an hour", Mark told Larry.

"…Um what? Why?" Larry was surprised.

"Just do it, and don't be late", Mark said before hanging up the phone.

Larry was now feeling scared, he had no idea why Mark wanted to see him. But, although Mark was a scary guy, he was still the son of Steve and Judy - the only people that Larry trusted. So he figured that he shouldn't fear Mark, and decided to go to the park and to see what he wanted.

Larry spent a lot of time on his own, gathering his thoughts, trying to figure out how he was going to make a future for himself with what his dad had left him. He stopped going to the office for a while, and he told the employees to take care of things while he takes a break. He used this time to go sit at his favourite coffee house, with the last of his business books. He hoped that whatever he had learned from these books would help him bring success to his dad's business. While he was reading, a little girl came up to Larry and just stared at him and smiled.

"Hey, what's your name?" Larry asked the girl.

"Allie", the girl replied.

"That's a really pretty name, Allie. I'm Larry", he told her.

"What are you reading?" Allie asked.

"Oh this, it's a just a boring book, see it doesn't have any pictures", Larry showed her the book.

"Is it for school?" she asked.

"Yes, it's for school", Larry laughed.

"Allie, there you are. Sorry if she was bothering you", the little girl's mother apologized to Larry.

"No it's okay, she wasn't bothering me. You have a lovely daughter. Bye Allie", Larry waved goodbye to Allie and her mother as they went back to their table.

"Bye Larry", Allie said as she blew him a kiss.

Larry smiled and his eyes started to fill with tears; sad tears that rolled down his cheeks on realizing that it wasn't just his parents that he lost that awful night. He also lost the little sister that he never got to see, the little sister that never gave him a goodbye kiss. As he looked at Allie and her mother sitting down at their table, he noticed a man sitting alone at a table in the corner. He was wearing sunglasses and a baseball cap, which made it difficult to see his face. Larry just realized that for the past week, he has been seeing this man at the same table just looking at Larry. The man noticed Larry was staring at him and left hurriedly. Larry never saw him again. Larry left soon after and headed back home. He arrived back to a quiet and empty home. He looked around the house, with most of the lights turned off. There was nobody there to ask him how he was, or how had his day been. Larry was becoming accustomed to stand in silence whenever he returned home, looking around the house and reminiscing about those exact things. Those things were now replaced by silence and emptiness. The sad part was that he was starting to get used to all the silence.

Larry decided to go back to the office, where the staff of fewer than 20 people had struggled to cope without their old boss. While Jack was there, he would do 90% of the work, which made his loss very challenging for the team. Larry was nowhere near as efficient as his dad, and he realized that they need to hire people to fill the gaping hole left by his dad. Larry placed ads for various job positions and was pessimistic about the chances of getting people to work for him, because he wasn't offering a decent salary and he thought nobody would want to work for a 17-year-old. A month passed and nobody had replied to his job offers. The shock came in the second month of him putting up the ads, when six people showed up within one week. Their names were Scott Sheppard, Coleen West, Susan Palmer, Frank Akerman, Jason Kay, and Sarah Phillips. They were all now the former colleagues of David Lawrence. Larry was surprised that they all came in at once. They didn't tell him that they used to work together. But Larry had no time to think about it, he just thanked his lucky stars that six random, or so he thought, well-qualified individuals wanted to work for him. He hired all of them on the spot, without knowing that he had just assembled the team that would build him his empire. Larry's new work force gathered the following week. And the team quickly realized how difficult a task it would be in turning around Larry's fortunes and making his business successful.

"…So, um…we should first…umm...start by…" Larry had no idea where to begin. He could barely do his own work when his dad was around. And as he paused, he looked around to see a team of older, more qualified, and experienced people, which he had to lead. He was starting to sweat and the team could clearly see that he was nervous.

"It's okay", Jason tried to calm him. "You are not really sure what to do right? Don't worry about it."

"Yeah he is right, don't worry", Sarah tried to ease his nerves as well, "You know, most of us didn't know what we were doing when we were your age too."

"I know, that's what my dad used to say…" Larry said with a sombre look on his face. Larry was missing his father.

"Look, you guys are way too qualified to be working for me. I totally understand if you guys wanna leave. You deserve better than to be working for an idiot like me. I'm sorry I wasted your time", Larry felt like giving up. He was thinking of closing the business and finding himself a job elsewhere.

"Larry, what you and your dad started is really good. Your business has potential of turning into something big, that's why we came to work for you. Granted, you don't know much about the business, but you just need a group of people around you who know what they are doing. And look around you Larry, that group is already here. As this business grows, so will your knowledge of business", Sarah was trying her best to convince Larry that he could lead this business.

The rest of the team agreed with Sarah. What Sarah said gave Larry that boost of confidence that he desperately needed.

"You're right. We can make this business big! I will become better at this! But I need your help. I know I'm supposed to be your boss but don't treat me like your boss. If I make a mistake, tell me! If I need to learn something, teach me! It might take some time but I WILL take this business to the top!" Larry was pumped. He also managed to pump up his team.

"Yeahhh!" yelled Jason, in his typical brash manner, as the rest of the team looked over at Jason.

"YEAH!" Larry yelled back at him, jumping out of his chair. That pumped the team even more. Their spirits were high and all of them, including Larry, believed that they could turn this business into something big. Amongst his new employees, Larry liked Sarah Phillips the most. Not only because he thought she was attractive, but also because he could clearly see that she was the smartest and most confident of the group. He made sure to find her alone before asking her a favour.

"Listen, I want you to lead this business for the first few months. I know I can lead this business, but not yet. Until that time comes I want you to make the major decisions, fill the role of my dad until I'm ready to take over", Larry told her.

"Wow, you want me to lead? Sure, I can do that", Sarah was surprised, but happy that Larry trusted her enough to ask this favour of her.

It was Larry's 18th birthday and the guys at work told him to take the day off and go enjoy his birthday. But it was his first birthday since he had lost his parents, and he didn't feel like celebrating. He didn't even have friends to celebrate with anyway, so he just went back home, ordered takeaway food and watched TV. The next day, he went early to work and saw that Jason and Sarah were already there.

"Hey it's the birthday boy, how are you?" Jason greeted him.

"I'm good, how are you guys?" Larry asked.

"We're good too. So…how was your birthday? Did you do anything special?" Sarah asked.

"No, I was home watching TV", Larry replied.

"What? You didn't go out with your friends or your girlfriend?" Sarah asked.

"No I don't have a girlfriend. Besides, I don't mind being alone, I enjoy it sometimes", Larry said with a chuckle.

Sarah and Jason felt sad for Larry. They just realized that he neither had friends, nor a social life. They had given him the day off expecting him to go and party. There was an awkward silence with Sarah and Jason for they did not know what to say to him. But Larry quickly changed the subject.

"…Um…you guys are here early. I was expecting to be the first one into work but you guys beat me", Larry told them.

"Yeah, Jason and I had some unfinished work from yesterday so we decided to come early today to finish it", Sarah replied.

"Oh, then I won't get in your way, I'm gonna be in my office if you guys need me", Larry said as he left the two of them.

"Oh my God! That's so sad. He spent his birthday alone", Sarah said to Jason, soon as Larry was out of sight.

"Yeah, I kinda feel sorry for him", Jason agreed.

"We have to do something for him, like throw a belated birthday party. We can have it at your beach house. What do you think?" Sarah asked Jason.

"That's not a bad idea. But you have seen MY parties! I don't know how to throw a birthday party for an 18-year-old. Should I bring a clown?" Jason questioned genuinely.

"He turned 18, not 8!" Sarah replied.

"I don't know, what am I supposed to do?" Jason was still clueless.

"Look, just make sure that there is plenty of food and drinks. I will bring the cake, and we will just hang out, we don't have to do anything special. But don't tell him, I will surprise him", Sarah explained.

"Alright, I can do that", Jason replied.

Sarah and Jason agreed to have a party for Larry. They told their close co-workers to meet up at Jason's beach house. Sarah was planning to surprise Larry. She told him that she was meeting someone to discuss business and that she wanted Larry to be with her. Given Larry's eagerness to learn more about business, he agreed to go with her to this meeting, not knowing that it was a surprise party for him. They arrived at the beach house and Larry was admiring how cool it looked. He wasn't even suspicious that a 'business meeting' was being held in a beach house. They went in and saw their co-workers sitting on the couch. When they saw Larry, they jumped up and shouted *"SURPRISE!"*

"…What?" Larry was confused.

"Surprise Larry! Nobody should spend their birthday alone, it's the least we can do for our boss", Sarah said as she gave Larry a kiss on the cheek.

Larry was left speechless, he could tell that they did this out of pity, but it was still the first time that anybody other than his parents have gone out of their way to cheer him up, and because of that, he was ultimately happy that they did that. He was also happy that he got a kiss from Sarah. The more time that he was spending with her, the more he was getting attracted to her.

"…Wow, I don't know what to say. Thanks guys." Larry told them.

"You're welcome boss. This place is open every weekend, and now that you know the place, you're free to come anytime", Jason told Larry.

"This is your place?" Larry asked.

"Yup, what do you think?" Jason asked.

"It looks really amazing. Seriously, I can come here anytime?" Larry asked.

"Only on the weekends", Jason replied.

"You said anytime", Sarah said.

"…Yeah, I meant anytime during the weekend", Jason said.

"Don't pay too much attention to what Jason is saying, I think he started the party way before we got here", Coleen laughed.

Larry enjoyed the surprise party; having felt for the first time in his life how it feels to hang out with a group of friends. He felt that these were people who wanted to be with him, and who actually liked him. It was what Larry desperately needed, now that his parents were gone. Jason's more subdued than usual party was winding down, and some of the co-workers were leaving. Larry was asking Sarah when they could leave because he wanted to go early to work the next day. Jason overheard him and insisted that both Larry and Sarah spend the night at his place and the next day, they would all go to work together.

"I don't mind, what do you think Larry?" Sarah asked.

"Umm…is there enough space?" Larry asked Jason.

"Yeah, I wouldn't have asked if there wasn't. Sarah can stay in the guest room, you can stay in my room, the other room is being renovated so I get the sofa bed in the living room", Jason replied.

"No I can't let you sleep on the sofa. It's your place. I should sleep on the sofa", Larry protested.

"It's not your choice boss. I never let the guests sleep on the sofa bed", Jason insisted.

The rest of the co-workers had left and the three of them were getting ready to go to sleep. Sarah was in her bed, trying to sleep when she heard noise from the TV in Jason's room. She went over to see that Larry was unable to sleep and he had turned on the TV.

"I'm sorry did I wake you? I couldn't sleep so I decided to watch some TV", Larry said.

"No its fine I didn't sleep yet. You mind if I stay and watch with you?" Sarah asked.

"Not at all", Larry replied.

Sarah got on the bed next to Larry, who was starting to feel a little flustered and his face became red. What made Larry feel more awkward was that Sarah had kept her shirt on, but taken off her pants and was just in her underwear. Sarah didn't mind since she didn't have any clothes with her for this surprise sleepover. But Larry was making sure that he maintains his gaze at the TV, in fear of his eyes wandering and looking at Sarah.

"Do you want me to move away from you?" Sarah asked.

"…Umm…no its fine…I…" Larry didn't know what to say.

"What? Do you have a crush on me or something?" Sarah joked.

"…Um…well you are really beautiful…how come you are single?" Larry asked.

"Oh, thank you! I'm divorced actually, and I never really thought about relationships after that. I just kept focusing on my career instead of men", Sarah explained. But she was in fact a widow.

Sarah had hoped to have a nice conversation with Larry, but Larry felt awkward the whole time she was there, and instead, the two of them just watched TV, in silence. Sarah could tell that Larry might be getting a little too attached to her so she made sure to tell him that there is no chance of a relationship between them because of their 7 year age difference.

"It's getting really late, I'm gonna go back to my room now", Sarah said.

"…Oh…yeah, have a good night", Larry replied.

"Listen, Larry, I just want to tell you something because I get the feeling that you might be attracted to me. Am I right?" Sarah asked.

"I just want to let you know so that you don't get your hopes up, but you are too young for me. I mean you just turned 18. And I'm not even looking for a relationship anyway so I just wanted to put that out there", Sarah was a bit too straight in telling Larry that there could never be anything between them. But it was just her strong personality that made it seem that she was a bit harsh.

"...Yeah I kinda had the feeling that there couldn't be anything between us. You're older than me, much smarter and so beautiful. You are way out of my league", Larry told Sarah.

Sarah didn't reply, partly because she was embarrassed by the nice words that Larry was saying to her. So she just told him goodnight and went back to her room.

PART FOUR

SARAH PHILLIPS

4

Sarah had been a colleague of David's for a few years and in that time, they had become really close friends. Just like David, she had a great mind for business and she also managed to make herself a nice living from doing what she loved. Sarah grew up in an upper middle class family. She was the middle child with one older and two younger brothers. Her mother had passed away when she was young and her father had raised them alone. Even though they had enough money, her father was very stingy when it came to money. He would never spoil his kids, especially Sarah, who grew to have a tough and stubborn personality from living in a household of just men. Not spoiling the kids was a strategy her father had employed to make them go out and work hard to make their own fortunes. But, her father took this strategy a little too extreme as even a birthday present was never bought for her. Sarah had enough of being rich but hadn't seen even a cent of that money. On her 18th birthday, she ran away from home and decided to find her own way. She got a job as a waitress in a diner. She knew that she was never going to make any fortune from this job, but she needed to start somewhere. Her strong personality was not her only asset, as she was blessed with beauty that was hard to resist for some men. One man in particular, was taken aback by her beauty.

"You're new here right? I have never seen you before", the man inquired.

"Yeah, I just started working here a couple of weeks ago. Are you ready to order?" Sarah asked him.

"What do you recommend?" The man asked again.

"I just told you I'm new here, I'm not too familiar with the menu. I will call my colleague who has been here longer, she can recommend something for you", Sarah replied.

"No that's okay…I will just have the cheeseburger with a diet coke, and your phone number", the man grinned.

"Why do you want my number?" Sarah knew, but she was just playing stupid.

"I would like to know you better", he replied.

"You know, I just moved out of my dad's house, and moved to the city, and got this glamorous job. I'm not really in a phase of my life where meeting men is a priority for me. I am sorry", Sarah said.

"What if you come work for me? I'm looking for a new assistant", the man replied.

"Really? What is it that you do?" Sarah asked.

"I'm an entrepreneur; I dabble in a bit of everything; real estate, restaurants, anything I can make money out of. Look, give me your number and I will set up an interview for you, unless you want to stay working in this diner", he told her.

"I guess I've got nothing to lose", Sarah wrote down her number on the napkin and handed it to him.

"It's nice to meet you…Sarah Hunter", he said as he read her name off the napkin. "I'm Matt Phillips. So, I will be giving you a call sometime next week and you can come for your interview."

Matt contacted Sarah and gave her the time and place for the interview. She went there, not really excited about the prospect of this job. What was driving her was her need to get out of her current job as a waitress. She had a drive in her to succeed, to be the best. A drive which was mainly fuelled by her desire to spite her brothers and her dad, who used to always put her down and say that she is not able to take care of herself. Matt informed her that he wanted someone to handle his bonds and stocks investment. Sarah didn't mind that, and there was nothing that she could have said in that interview that would have changed Matt's mind about hiring her, because he was already infatuated with her. They agreed on the salary and living accommodation, and she was hired by Matt that same day. She was a real hard worker, and she was impressing Matt week after week by her intelligence and her natural knack for business. He kept trying to get closer to her in hopes of having more than a professional relationship, but Sarah wasn't interested. After just a couple of months at the job, she got promoted and she was really starting to make a name for herself, which unfortunately for her, made it easier for her dad to finally track her down after a yearlong hunt. Sarah was walking in the hallways at work when she was surprised to see her dad standing in the middle of the hallway. She didn't say anything at first, and she just stood there looking at him.

"…Sarah, honey, I am so happy I finally managed to see you. I have been looking for you for a while. Whatever it is that I did to make you run away, I'm sorry. And I'm so proud to see what you have managed to do for yourself", he said.

"How did you find me?" She finally responded.

"I heard about you, I heard about a big shot new business woman named Sarah Hunter. I didn't doubt for a second that it was my daughter. I'm so proud of you. I knew you would make it", he said.

"Proud? You shouldn't be proud. It's all my own hard work. You had nothing to do with it", Sarah snapped at him.

Her shocked dad remained silent. Matt was calling her on her cell phone, and just seeing his number flash on the screen, an idea popped in her head, an idea that she thought would help distance her from her dad for good.

"…It's my boss…who is my fiancé too. I'm going to marry him, and I'm going to take his name. That way, you won't hear about Sarah Hunter anymore", Sarah said.

"…You're getting married?!" Her dad asked in surprise.

"Yes, so I'm kinda glad you did come to see me, because now you can say goodbye to your daughter Sarah Hunter, because she won't exist anymore", Sarah said.

Her dad was speechless again, and felt heartbroken.

"Have a nice life Mr. Hunter." Sarah, as cruelly as she could have, ended her last meeting ever with her dad with those words. After she said that, she calmly walked away, turning her back on the man whom she felt had his back turned on her, her whole life. The idea of saying she was going to marry Matt was starting to seem like not a bad idea to her. Since she started working for Matt, every other guy that worked there tried to flirt with her. And she hated that because she felt like she wasn't respected. So becoming the boss's wife would make those guys show her some respect. She never felt repulsed by Matt whatsoever, and even though he was 10 years older than her, he was a fairly good-looking guy. But she just kept turning him down because she was never interested in a relationship. But having thought about the benefits of being with Matt, she decided to play a little game with Matt, to show him that it was time for him to make his move.

"Hey boss, I finished my work for today, do you mind if I leave early?" Sarah told Matt.

"Is there a problem? Are you okay?" Matt asked.

"I just feel like I'm coming down with a cold", Sarah said.

"Oh, yeah sure you can leave. If you want I could go to the pharmacy after work and bring you some medicine", Matt was trying to take advantage of any situation that would allow him to see her after work.

"That would be nice, thanks," Sarah said.

Matt was surprised to say the least. He didn't know if she was finally opening the door for him to get closer to her, or if she really was that sick. He was excited nonetheless, and he also left early to go get the medicines for Sarah. After what he perceived as a successful attempt, Matt decided to try his luck and ask to see Sarah again after she got better, where he decided to straight out ask her to be in a relationship with him.

"Listen, Sarah. I'm really attracted to you", Matt said.

"You don't say", Sarah sarcastically replied.

"I was wondering if perhaps you changed your mind about being in a relationship", Matt chuckled.

"You're 30, I'm 20. Don't you think you are too old for me?" Sarah asked him.

"But that's one of the reasons I'm so attracted to you, you don't act your age at all. Yeah I'm a little older, but that just means that I'm serious about a relationship and the prospect of marriage", Matt explained.

"Wow, I haven't said yes to a relationship and you're already asking to marry me", Sarah said.

"No that's not what I meant. I just meant that I'm looking for a serious relationship that would EVENTUALLY lead to marriage", Matt said.

"I know what you meant. I was just messing with you. Okay." Sarah said.

"Okay what?" Matt asked.

"Okay, I will be you girlfriend slash eventual wife", Sarah joked.

Sarah was neither hating nor loving the fact that she had gotten in a relationship with Matt. It was exactly how she was feeling when she first came to work for him. Because she was not entirely stable in her life, she felt that if she got married, she could focus more on improving her professional career. For that reason, she figuratively stepped on the gas in order to quickly move their relationship forward. Matt never brought up marriage again since he had already mentioned it at the start of their relationship. So Sarah kindly reminded him of that issue by telling him that she was in love with him, and that she was ready to get married. They were just hollow words, but because Matt was head over heels for her, he believed her, and Matt wasn't going to waste any time because finally, the girl he had been crazy for, for 2 years said she wanted to marry him, and shortly thereafter, they got married. It was a small ceremony, filled mainly with Matt's friends, family, and employees. None of Sarah's family was present, mainly because she didn't invite any of them.

"Good morning Mrs. Phillips", the secretary greeted her as Sarah Phillips for the first time. Her work ethic and desire to improve her professional career was evident by the fact that she told Matt to postpone their honeymoon trip for another time. After subtly convincing Matt to speed up their relationship, she took a few steps back after getting married, and she was now treating Matt exactly how she was at the beginning; indifferent.

"We have a really busy schedule coming up. Don't you think it's best to delay it?" Sarah tried to convince Matt to postpone their honeymoon.

"But I thought you were excited to go on a cruise?" Matt replied.

"We can go on a cruise anytime. We should focus on our work first. Didn't you say you were meeting with some stock broker next week?" Sarah said.

"Yeah, I guess you are right. Whatever you think is best", Matt said, "Yeah, I'm meeting the guy next week, his name is David, something, I forgot. Are you sure you can't make it?" Matt asked.

"I have a lot of other stuff to take care of, maybe if you meet him again another time I can make it", Sarah said.

Matt went to his meeting with David Lawrence, and Matt couldn't believe his luck; he had just gotten married to the girl of his dreams, and now he felt like he had met the man who would help him become a millionaire. Matt had heard about David, and how he was considered a genius when it came to stocks and investing, and Matt wanted to hire him as an advisor. Matt was a bit disappointed that Sarah couldn't be with them. He insisted that Sarah meet him whenever she had the chance, and she agreed to meet him the next time Matt went to see him.

"Honey, this is him, this is the guy I was telling you about. David, this is my wife Sarah", Sarah walked into Matt's office to see David sitting there, and Matt introduced the two.

"It's nice to meet you David", Sarah said.

"Likewise", David replied politely.

As Matt and David were talking, Sarah was sitting quietly, mesmerized by David's charm. She wanted to get close to him by any means possible. After the meeting, she asked for David's number so that they could discuss business as well, if Matt was ever busy.

"What did I tell you?" Matt told Sarah after David left.

"You are right, the guy is good," Sarah replied. Matt had inadvertently introduced her to the man who would take her away from him, but it would not be David's fault. Sarah called David the following week and wanted to meet with him, alone. He was free and agreed to meet her again. Sarah chose the place, and she was there sipping her coffee when David arrived and sat at the table with her. After the normal greetings, he went straight to the point.

"So what did you want to discuss?" David asked her.

"I don't know, I want to know more about you", Sarah replied.

"Oh so this is a social meeting, not a business meeting", David said.

"Yeah you could say that", Sarah replied.

"I'm sorry but I'm married", David told her.

"So? I'm married too, that doesn't mean that we can't sit and talk", Sarah said.

She convinced David that there was nothing wrong with what they were doing. She wanted more than just to talk, but seeing how quickly David brought up the fact that he was married, she thought he wasn't going to be easy to seduce. She planned instead to just befriend him, and then make her move once she left Matt. Sarah never used sweet words when talking with Matt. It was not a marriage of love, like Matt believed it to be. It was a sham, it was just for show. Having been married for a year now, Sarah felt like this marriage has outlived its usefulness. She got his name, she settled down, and now she wanted to end it. Another reason she wanted it to end was because she was now attracted to another man. Living up to her original last name, Sarah was a hunter, if she saw something she wanted, she would go after it. And now, she wanted David. She told David that she wanted to work with him many times. He even introduced her to his closest colleague, Jason Kay. But there were no job openings available that David could help her with. During this period, where Sarah spent most of her time with David and Jason, Matt was feeling left out, and he was a sensitive soul, he was starting to believe that Sarah might not be in love with him.

"I love you", Matt said to Sarah as they were lying in bed.

Sarah was busy reading; she just smiled and gave Matt a pat on the cheek. She didn't reply back with 'I love you too'. The next day at work, Matt found out that he needed to go on a business trip to another state. He begged Sarah to come with him, because he had the feeling that if he left her for 2 weeks, he would come back to see her gone. Sarah, of course, declined to go with him. Matt reluctantly left for his business trip, and when he would return, his worst fear would come true. Sarah saw those two weeks as the perfect opportunity to end her marriage and close this chapter of her life with Matt. Even though she didn't love Matt, she still didn't hate him. And she knew that it will break his heart if she told him to his face that she wanted a divorce. She saw it best to get the paperwork done for the divorce while he was away, and have her lawyer deliver the news to him. The divorce papers were done, and they were waiting on Matt's desk. She made sure to hand in her resignation papers before Matt left, to give herself time to get it done before he comes back, and without him knowing. With that out of the way, she called David after her resignation was complete because her plan wasn't finished yet.

"Hey Sarah, are you okay? You sounded serious on the voice message you left", Sarah left a voicemail for David, and he returned the call when he had some free time.

"I got fired!" Sarah lied.

"What? Why?" David asked.

"I had a big fight with Matt, and he fired me, he doesn't want to see me again. He wants a divorce!" Sarah continued her story.

"I'm so sorry to hear that", David hadn't spoken to Matt in months, and he didn't even know that Matt wasn't even in New York, so he believed her fake story.

"You have to help me, please, you have to get me a job with you", Sarah pleaded with David.

"Okay, I will see what I can do", David replied.

Because David was very well liked by his boss, he managed to get Sarah a job with them, but the paperwork was going to take awhile, which Sarah didn't mind as it gave her time to go apartment hunting. And with that, she had successfully cut the cord with Matt Phillips. As quickly as her marriage to Matt happened, it also ended, and she believed him to be out of her life now, and she could start a new chapter in her life. When Matt returned, he called Sarah but she had changed her number. He went home but didn't see her there, or any of her stuff. He was starting to worry now, he was tired from his flight and he wasn't able to sleep, and his 2-week business trip had been a complete failure. He went to work the next day, with a scruffy beard which he wasn't bothered to shave, and in a regular shirt and pants as oppose to his usual classy suit. He walked, not interested to talk to anyone, and he went to his office where his secretary told him that Sarah quit. Matt's heart sank, the look on his face made it difficult for her give him the news that was even worse than her quitting. Instead, she just told him to go to his office so that he can see for himself. He slowly stuttered towards his office, just like a death row inmate making his slow walk to his execution. He had a feeling of what was about to come. It was just a short time ago when he had felt like he was the luckiest man in the world. But it appeared that his luck had run out. He went into his office and saw an envelope on his desk. His hands were shaking, his heart was beating faster than ever, and the stress and jetlag from his long flight only added to his stressed state of mind. He was trying to open the envelope but because his hands were shaking, he accidently tore it open. The only words that he read were 'dissolution of marriage'. Matt put his hand on his chest, he was trying to breath but he couldn't. He began feeling lightheaded, with a weird stinging pain shooting up his left arm. His whole office began to spin, and he collapsed on the floor. A couple of employees heard the thud and came rushing in. They went to check on him and he wasn't breathing, they called 911 and he was rushed to the hospital. Attempts to resuscitate him were futile, and he was pronounced dead only minutes after arriving at the hospital. The official cause of death was listed as a heart attack. But, a more accurate cause of death would have been a broken heart.

Sarah heard the news the next day, and she was sad, but not heartbroken. She still went about adjusting into her new workplace. David also heard the news of Matt's death, and he went to offer his condolences to Sarah.

"I heard what happened. I'm sorry", David said.

"Thank you", Sarah replied.

"When is the funeral? Tell me when you are going, I will come with you", David said.

"No, I won't be going, I just can't." Sarah said. But the reason that she wasn't going was because she was embarrassed by David's question. She had no idea when or where the funeral will be, she wasn't intending to go to his funeral because she saw Matt as a part of her past now, and there was no need for her to remain attached to him.

"You don't have to stay at work today. You can go home, it's okay", David told her.

"No I want to stay here. It will help keep my mind of it", Sarah said.

David went alone to the funeral. Even though he didn't get to know Matt well enough, he still felt obliged to go and pay his respects. That gave Sarah enough time to get better acquainted with her new colleagues.

"So I'm Jason, you know that because you already met me. That's Susan, Colleen, Scott and Frank. This is our little group, we're not talented, good looking, or smart. But we make a lot of money", Jason Kay took it upon himself to introduce Sarah to her new colleagues.

"After that introduction, let me just say sorry. But you're gonna be working with us so you have to get used to this clown", Susan told Sarah.

Sarah liked her new colleagues; she felt that she could fit in well with them. But her ever illusive target, David, would never give in to her many attempts of getting close to him, so they remained close friends instead.

PART FIVE

DOWNHILL

5

Whether it's a coincidence or not is uncertain at this point, but ever since Sarah came into David's life, things went sour. Work-wise, the team had gotten stronger with the addition of Sarah. But David's close bond with this new and attractive colleague did not go down well with his wife Jennifer. Slowly but surely, the damage she is doing to their marriage was going to reach the point of no repair. After the big party that they held in David's honour, David became a different person. As if something happened that night that turned him into someone else; he began to slack off at work and he became negligent with his wife and daughter. Things that were considered unthinkable actions for a guy like David.

"What's keeping you busy?" His wife confronted him about his changed behaviour. "We don't get to see you anymore. You keep telling me you are busy with work, and yesterday they call to ask about you, saying you haven't been to work in a week! What's going on?"

David didn't know what to say to her, he wanted to tell her the truth. But the truth would kill him, so he just remained silent.

"It's Sarah isn't it? You are seeing her aren't you? Is that what you are doing with your time now?" Jennifer told him.

David slapped his wife. "Don't you dare accuse me of cheating on you again! How many times have I told you, Ṣarah is just a friend, there is just a lot of work for me to do now at my job and it's making me lose my mind. I don't need you to make things worse with your jealousy and stupidity", he told her.

It was obvious to her that David was hiding something. David had a soft spot for Sarah, and his wife knew that. It wasn't the first time that she had suspected something more between them, but it was the first time that David had reacted violently. Days passed and his marriage was not getting any better. He returned home one night to find the house empty, with no sign of his wife or daughter. The only thing he could see was a letter set on the dining table. His wife had left with their daughter and she wanted a divorce. David finally realized that he was treating them badly, but he was too busy to realize that in time. She had left now, and she wasn't answering his calls.

"I'm sorry, please come back. I swear I'm working on a new project, please understand that. I'm sorry I have been neglecting you, and I am sorry I hit you...please forgive me."

Even voice messages that he left went unanswered, and he came to the conclusion that it would be best to give her the divorce that she wanted. David wasn't even allowed to see his daughter during the divorce proceedings. The divorce was finalized, but what hurt him most was that the judge ruled that his now ex-wife will take full custody of their daughter. Jennifer made sure to take a picture of the bruise the she got when David slapped her, and it was evidence that David could not deny, which made the judge rule in Jennifer's favour.

"What's going on with you Dave?" David's boss asked.

David went to work after missing a couple of days due to the divorce and the stress that he was under, and his boss wanted to check on him.

"I'm sorry sir. I just have a lot of things on my mind at the moment, with the divorce and everything. Sorry I have been slacking off", David apologized for his tardiness.

"I'm sad to hear about your divorce from Jennifer, I really thought that you guys were perfect for each other. I know what it's like going through a divorce, it can be tough. But I never let it get in the way of my work, so you shouldn't either. Because you are important to us and I like you, I will just give you a warning this time. Make sure you pick yourself up because it will be even worse to lose your wife and your job", his boss warned.

"I'm sorry sir, I won't let you down", David replied.

His boss left David's office to let him get back to his work. But he couldn't do that, as he got a call just a few minutes later.

"Hey Dave, are we meeting later today because we got a lot of stuff to run by you", the caller said.

"Yeah okay, I'm just finishing of my work and then I will meet you guys afterwards", David sighed in exhaustion.

Larry was starting to grow exponentially now that he has support at work. But it was Mark who planted the seed in him that was now starting to grow and strengthen Larry's character. After that meeting in the park, the two formed an unbreakable bond, with Mark taking up the mantle of being Larry's guardian. Nobody knows Mark's story, he was a book whose cover was worn out, but its pages were empty. Larry didn't ask him why a 35 year old retired Marine was living in his parent's basement, or why he had a wedding ring but there was no sign of a wife or kids. Larry was not scared to see him anymore; he was starting to like him. Mark had the allure of a real life superhero to him. Mark called Larry one evening and told him to visit him in the basement of his parent's house. Larry arrived at Steve's home and went inside to find the house empty. He heard the sound of metal clanging coming from the basement and what sounded like classical music. He went down to the basement to see Mark drenched in sweat from working out.

"Looks intense!" Larry exclaimed.

Mark dropped the dumbbell and gathered his breath and walked towards Larry.

"Punch me!" Mark ordered Larry.

Stunned by this request, Larry didn't say anything.

"You're too soft, you gotta learn how to fight, I won't always be there to defend you. You need to learn to take care of yourself. Punch me!" Mark said as he shoved Larry.

Larry was still confused, but not scared; he really did feel that Mark just wanted him to toughen up; something that Larry wanted to do. Without saying anything, Larry took a swing at Mark, a swing which was easily deflected as Mark threw Larry to the ground. He then picked him up off the floor and told him to try again. Larry was getting pumped up; adrenaline was rushing through his body. They sparred for an hour, with Larry never actually landing that punch on Mark.

"You need some work! Come by next time!" Mark told Larry as he picked up his towel, ready to leave.

"Its this music man! I cant concentrate! Who works out while listening to classical music?"

As he was going up the stairs, Mark stopped to answer Larry.

"Habanera...it helps me focus." Mark answered as he closed the stereo and left Larry alone.

Larry laid on the bench, not ready to leave the basement because he was still catching his breath. Nonetheless, he enjoyed that surprise training session, and they would have a few more over time. These sparring sessions would help Larry toughen up physically and mentally, and they will mould him into the man that he is destined to become.

PART SIX

BUILDING HIS EMPIRE

6

With Sarah's help, Larry was starting to fit into the role of the boss at work. But the business was still struggling in terms of progress. This prompted one of the six people that came to work for Larry, to question his decision to answer Larry's job ad.

"I knew this was gonna be a risky career move, I'm starting to regret I actually took it", said Scott.

"Of course it was risky to work for a 17-year-old. But we still came anyway, because we knew that we would have a great mind behind us. It's always hardest in the beginning, there is potential here for things to become better, you have to be patient", Susan tried to reason with him, but Scott's mind was set.

"I thought there was potential too, but once inside the company, I saw how hopeless the 'boss' is and realized that this wasn't worth the risk. Tell your dumb boss that I'm quitting, and I'm going back to my old job", Scott saw no future in Larry's business and decided to jump ship while he still could, because he was the oldest of the new employees, he didn't want to waste his time.

Sarah broke the news to Larry the next day, who was disappointed with himself mostly, because he felt that he failed as a boss.

"He quit! It's my fault isn't it? I'm not cut out to lead a business", Larry was blaming himself. He tried calling Scott to try to convince him to change his decision but he wasn't answering.

"Forget about him! You said to teach you when you needed to learn something. Here is a lesson - always look for the positive in every situation. You managed to convince 5 people that you are able to lead this business, only one guy quit!" Sarah said.

"You're right, you guys are still here", Larry replied

"Yeah, and I think I might know a perfect guy to replace Scott. He's a friend of mine, his name is David Lawrence", Sarah said.

"Great, if you think he would be good for us, call him", replied Larry.

Sarah talked to David about the job but he declined her offer. With all the stress that David was going through, it was understandable why he declined to take on a risky job. Sarah decided it was best not to hire anyone to fill Scott's place because she believed in the strength of the other colleagues who are still here.

Jason called Larry into his office, where he saw the rest of the team huddled around Jason's computer. Jason had taken charge of drawing up a new direction for the business, and he wanted to get Larry's opinion.

"Larry, we have come up with a great plan for our business. Tell us what you think?" Jason said.

Larry was standing over Jason's desk and looking at his computer. He read the summary of the plan and was very happy with it, even though there was some stuff that he didn't understand, but was too embarrassed to tell them. But he had faith that the guys knew what they were doing, and he gave Jason and the team approval to go ahead with the plan, but he wanted to change the new name that they came up with for the business.

"What's wrong with Larry Stone Enterprises?" Jason asked. "I think it's really catchy."

"Hang on…" Larry leaned over Jason to use the keyboard. He scrolled over *'Larry Stone'* and deleted it and replaced it with just two letters: JL.

"JL? Why are you naming it after Jennifer Lopez?" Jason joked.

"Jack and Lindsey", Coleen jumped in, "Those were his parents' names. I like it. I think that's a really nice touch."

Larry, now knowing that nothing could happen between him and Sarah, felt more comfortable to be around her, and thought she could still be a great friend. He asked her one day after work if she wanted to go hang out, but, she told him that she already had other plans. She did however, set up another day for them to hang out. Larry instead called Jason whom he already knew was out with his friends, to see if there was room for one more. Jason enjoyed Larry's company, and he invited him over to hang out with him and his friends even though they were much older than him. Having no friends besides his parents when he was growing up, and then having absolutely nobody after they died, Larry was happy that for the first time in his life, he could pick up the phone and call somebody to hang out with. He was also happy that things were going well at work. Jason and Sarah were really on a roll in terms of making progress for the company. At the same time, Larry was learning a lot just by being around them and seeing them work. He was still however confused, as to why these well-qualified people had come to work for him. In his desperation to hire people as quickly as possible, he never got the chance to ask them that question. But the time finally came for him to put Jason and Sarah on the spot.

"No Larry, we have to set up a network for us to expand this business. We need connections. Since we are the little fish, we need to attract the big fish. That's how we get our name out there", Jason was explaining to Larry.

"You guys sure know how to handle things. I'm surprised why you guys ever came to work for me. You guys could easily go anywhere you wanted to, why me and my business?" Larry finally asked Sarah and Jason the question that had been bugging him ever since he had hired them.

Jason and Sarah were sideswiped by that question. They didn't know how to answer him without giving away too much. Jason remained quiet, looking at Sarah, hoping that she would answer instead.

"I really like to challenge myself. Instead of going to work at something that's already big, I would rather work at something small and make it big. For me, that is more satisfying." That was partially true. "Plus, I heard about your parents' accident and that a 17-year-old was left to take care of his dad's business. So I have to admit there was also sympathy as well in my decision to come work for you." This part of her answer was a lie.

Having given a somewhat detailed answer to Larry's question, Sarah and Larry now looked at Jason to give his reasons for coming to work for Larry.

"I was fired from my job. I wanted something quick. Your ad was the first one I saw." Jason was obviously lying, but it was believable enough for Larry.

"Hey what are you doing tonight?" Sarah asked Larry.

"Nothing", Larry replied.

"You wanna go have coffee after work?" Sarah asked.

"Yeah that would be great", Larry said.

Sarah kept her word when she re-scheduled a hangout with Larry, and they left work to go the coffee house nearby. The two sat down and the first thing that they were talking about was work, mainly because Larry brought it up.

"You really are a workaholic aren't you?" Sarah said with a smile. "We finished work and you are still talking about work."

"I can't help it, I'm addicted now", Larry joked.

"You have to relax your mind though. It's good that you are always thinking about work. But at the same time, you need to switch off from time to time, otherwise you will just stress yourself", Sarah advised him.

"Yeah, I guess you're right, "Larry said.

"I wanna know more about your parents, tell me about them", Sarah asked.

"Well, I don't know how to start. Nobody asked me to talk about my parents before", Larry said.

"I'm sorry, you don't have to talk about it if you don't want to", Sarah quickly apologized.

"No, it's fine. I just think the best way to describe my parents is to say that they were my friends too…they were my only friends…the night of the accident…when the hospital called me and told me what happened, I just fell to the ground and started crying…wish I had died with them, I was supposed to be with them. But…I thought about what my life goal has been when they were alive. I always wanted to make them proud…and I can still do that…I guess, that's why I always talk about work…I want to be successful…I want to make them proud", Larry, for the first time was opening up to someone about his feelings. And Sarah was happy that he trusted her enough to be able to talk about such a personal topic.

"But I will never move on until I see justice served", Larry told her. Sarah was surprised by how his demeanour changed when he said that.

"What do you mean?" Sarah asked.

"I found out that there was a witness to the accident. They said that another car caused them to crash, and then fled the scene. The police didn't do anything with this information. They didn't care to look for that person. Well, I care…and I'm not gonna stop looking for this person. And when I find them, I will make sure that they will get what they deserve", Larry proclaimed.

Sarah believed that Larry was serious about his pursuit of the person who had killed his parents. She felt that he could do something evil if he ever found that person.

"Well I think that you are really strong to make it through that tragedy on your own", Sarah said.

"To be fair, I wasn't totally alone. My parent's friends visited me from time to time to check on me. I owe them a lot. I did also get close with their oldest son, but I don't see him anymore. And now of course, I have you guys", Larry said as Sarah smiled. Even though the subject was uncomfortable for Sarah to listen to, she still wanted to know how Larry felt about what happened to his parents. And she was happy that he opened up to her and no one else. She felt that she had gotten closer to Larry.

Larry and Sarah's hangouts became a weekly thing, the two were starting to get really close, with Sarah also opening up to Larry about her life. One of those weeks however, Sarah declined their now weekly rendezvous, because she had to go out with some friends. Larry didn't mind, and he tried to see if Jason was free but he also declined. Again, Larry wasn't upset. But instead of staying at home, he thought he would go to his favourite coffee shop. As he was on his way, for no apparent reason, he decided to try something different and go try a new coffee shop. He came across one that had recently opened, so he decided to try it out. He walked in the coffee house which was fairly bigger than the other one that he always goes to. As he was looking around the place, he was surprised to see Sarah, Jason, Frank, Coleen and Susan sitting together.

"Hey, what are you guys doing here?" Larry asked them.

They all remained silent. Especially Jason, who wasn't the best at lying, and they all looked over at Sarah to bail them out.

"My friends cancelled their plans and these guys said they were gonna go over some work so I decided to join them. Sorry we didn't tell you", Sarah explained to Larry.

"That's alright. I guess it was still meant to be that I join this impromptu meeting because it was by chance that I came here. Besides, you saved an empty seat right at the head of the table, just where the boss is supposed to sit", Larry said referring to the sixth chair at the table which was empty. "Or is someone sitting here?" Larry asked.

"No boss, have a seat", Jason told him.

But there was someone sitting at the head of the table, and that person left as soon as they had seen Larry walk into the coffee house. Larry wasn't upset that they were meeting without him. On the contrary, he was happy to see that they were still working during their free time.

"Whose glasses are these? They are pretty huge!" Larry asked, referring to the sunglasses that were left at his seat.

"Umm, yeah those are mine." Jason said as he took them away. But they belonged to the person that was sitting there before Larry. The group were meeting with someone that for some reason, didn't want to be seen by Larry. Jason would return those glasses to the person the next time they met, and Larry would remain oblivious to the teams secret meetings with that person.

PART SEVEN

MR. LARRY STONE

7

Three years passed and the business had progressed well. They were on the road towards something big. But they would encounter a hurdle that nobody saw coming. Frank had heard of a prominent businessman that has come to the city. He planned to expand his already large company and that could spell the end for JL Enterprises.

"This is bad", said Frank, "This guy couldn't have picked another city. We don't have the resources to rival this guy."

"Try to contact him, maybe we can work out some sort of deal. Jason and Sarah are good at dealing with people. See if you can arrange a meeting with him", Larry set the task of dealing with the rival to Jason and Sarah. Their efforts, however, were unsuccessful. They spent weeks trying to get in contact with this businessman but they would always be denied by his secretary, saying that he doesn't have the time to meet anyone.

"The guy wouldn't even meet with us. We sent emails, we called, but the guy is just ignoring us. I think that's it for us, we have to find a new direction for our business because we will lose if we compete with this guy", Jason conceded defeat to their new rival.

"He's ignoring us, huh? If that's how he wants to play then let me deal with this guy in my own way", Larry said.

"What are you gonna do Larry? You sound serious. You're not gonna send him a horse's head are you?" Jason joked.

"No I don't know how to get a horse's head, so I will have to send him something else", Larry replied in similar light-hearted manner. But what he was intending certainly wasn't light-hearted. A few weeks pass and to the astonishment of everyone in the company, except for Larry, the businessman cancelled the plans for his new venture in the city. The next day, everyone was still staggered by the news, and when Larry went to work, everyone looked at him wondering how he had managed to deal with the guy.

"Seriously Larry, What the hell did you do?!" A shocked Jason asked.

"Nothing, just marked my territory", Larry calmly responded. "Now, with that out of the way, let's carry on with business."

It was clear now to everybody that this was not the same shy and quiet Larry that they first met. His personality had become stronger, he became much smarter, and he was now the real leader of the company. He never did tell Jason what he did to scare away the rich businessman. He kept it a secret. In time however, Jason will learn what this secret was, the hard way. This new assertive and commanding Larry was starting to win over Sarah. They had been good friends now for a few years, and despite the 7-year age gap, she was starting to feel that there might be the makings of a perfect relationship for her. Instead of waiting to see if Larry still had feelings towards her, she decided to make the first move and ask Larry out.

"Hey Larry, what are you doing tonight? It's been a long time since we hung out. I was wondering if you wanted to do something", Sarah asked him.

"Sure, that sounds great. Do you have anything in mind?" Larry asked.

"How about just hanging out at your place? It's been a long time since you cooked anything for me", Sarah said.

Larry was getting the feeling that Sarah was up to something. Even though the idea of them being together was out of his head ever since she bluntly told him that there is no chance years ago, he felt that she was trying to make a move on him.

"Yeah, I don't mind. Just let me know when you are on your way." Larry said.

Later that night, Sarah arrived at Larry's place and Larry was preparing dinner. Sarah wanted to help, but Larry insisted that he doesn't need help, so she just sat in the living room watching the music channel on TV. When Larry finished cooking, he set up the table and the two of them sat to have dinner.

"Wow, this chicken pasta looks nice", Sarah complimented Larry's cooking.

"Thanks." Larry replied.

Larry saw that Sarah wasn't her usual talkative self that night. She seemed shy and he felt like she was keeping something from him.

"So, what brings you here tonight?" Larry asked her. Sarah was surprised by that question. It just showed how much Larry has matured, and how the tables had turned. It was just a few years ago that Sarah was shooting down any hopes Larry had of getting in a relationship with her. Now it was Larry asking Sarah to reveal whatever feelings he felt she was showing him the past few weeks.

"…I just thought we could hang out", Sarah replied.

Larry just raised his eyebrow and smiled. "I feel like you want to say something. Go ahead, don't be shy." Larry told her.

"YOU are telling me not to be shy? I must not be very good at hiding my feelings then huh?" Sarah said.

"Hey, I wasn't good at hiding my feelings towards you before also, you were able to tell. And now, I can tell", Larry said.

Sarah just looked down, with her cheeks starting to turn red. She remained quiet, with the only sound now coming from the TV that she left on.

"So, you like me?" Larry asked her.

Sarah with her head down and her cheeks still bright red nodded yes.

"Since when? I thought I was too young for you", Larry said.

"…You have really changed lately, you seem more mature…I now realize that the age difference isn't as big a problem as I thought…and I'm willing to look past it…if you don't hate me now", Sarah told him.

"Hate you?" Larry asked.

"I turned you down before and now I'm the one that's…I don't know…I just feel bad about it", Sarah explained.

"I wasn't upset when you turned me down. I thought you had good reason. I don't hate you for that. I still like you…I have always liked you", Larry confessed.

With both of them now having expressed their feelings towards each other, fate gave them a helping hand as well, as the song that was being played at the moment on TV was Shania Twain's '*When You Kiss Me.*' Sarah was now blushing again. But this time, she had held her head up and was looking into Larry's eyes, smiling. Larry was looking back at her with a similar smile."(*You are the one, I think I'm in love…)*" As Shania Twain was serenading them movingly, it felt like an eternity that they were staring at each other and smiling. But it was only for a few seconds, and in those few seconds they both knew that they had fallen in love with each other.

"…Larry…" Sarah said.

"It's okay", Larry interrupted her," You don't have to say anything." Larry said.

Sarah went on to spend the night at Larry's place. And the next day, when they went to work together, they made it official that they were now in a relationship, by walking into work while holding hands.

"What is this? When did this happen?"A surprised Jason greeted them. "Are you for real?"

"Yup", Larry replied while looking at Sarah.

"Wow, I gotta say I'm surprised. But I am still happy for you guys. Congrats!" Jason said.

"Thanks", Sarah replied.

"…So when's the baby?" Jason joked.

"Dude, you gotta know when a joke is too far", Larry said as he gave Jason a friendly punch on the shoulder.

"Was that inappropriate?" Jason asked.

"Just a bit ", Sarah replied.

"Sorry...I guess then you're not gonna name the baby after me?" Jason joked again. Sarah and Larry just eyed Jason.

"Alright alright, that was the last joke I swear. I gotta go to my office", Jason said, leaving quickly.

After Larry and Sarah got in a relationship, they began distancing themselves from the rest of the group. Larry stopped going over to Jason's place, and most of his time was spent with his new girlfriend. Jason had known Sarah the longest, and after a month passed he decided to have a big brother talk with Larry about his new girlfriend.

"Hey boss, you busy?" Jason said as he walked into Larry's office.

"No I'm actually bored, come entertain me", Larry joked.

"I told you guys, stop talking to me like I'm a clown", Jason replied.

"I'm just messing with you. Have a seat", Larry said.

"So, how is your girlfriend?" Jason asked.

"Oh man, I'm in love", Larry replied.

"Really? You haven't been going out for long ", Jason said.

"I don't know what to tell you man, she is just incredible. She's smart, funny and so gorgeous, I feel really lucky," Larry said.

"That's great. I'm happy for you…but, just be careful", Jason warned.

"What do you mean?" Larry was puzzled.

"Well, you are starting to change since you have been with her. I mean, you don't even come over for the weekends, I had to have this talk with you at work, I don't see you anymore", Jason said.

"I'm sorry man, it's just that we are going out a lot. Do you know she likes salsa? We went dancing a couple of weeks ago", Larry said.

"I didn't know you could do salsa", Jason said.

"I didn't either! You are right, I'm changing, but I'm changing for the better. I'm a man in love. I think you are just jealous I managed to get the hot girl and you didn't", Larry said.

"No man, I'm single for life, that's my motto. Kill me if I ever get into a relationship. But, if you're really happy, then who am I to give you advice. Congratulations man."

"Thanks man, and we will try to come over some time", Larry replied.

Sarah was going through this same topic in her head, because she never really had someone who cared about her like Jason cared about Larry. She was asking herself similar questions about her new relationship with Larry. She only had one relationship before this, and it was her marriage to Matt Phillips. But unlike her relationship with Matt, she had actually fallen in love with Larry. This time around, there were no advantages that she wanted to reap from the relationship. She wanted to be with Larry because she loved him. But on the other hand, there was an advantage from distancing Larry from the rest of the group, and she was the one that would always decide to go somewhere else every time Larry suggests they go over to Jason. Larry and Sarah would go on to have a loving relationship, but they were drifting further and further away from the rest of the group.

PART EIGHT

JL ENTERPRISES

8

A business that had started with just a dad and son duo had now become a powerful empire that had taken over New York. Larry still has the same 5 people that he had hired to work for him, except now, they form the board of his company, with of course much better salaries than when they first started. Sarah was the most influential amongst the board members, not only because she was the best, but because she was now Larry's fiancée. Along with Sarah, Jason Kay had the biggest influence in the growth of JL Enterprises and he was now Larry's right-hand man. Larry grew to become an authoritative boss, and his stern approach provided for volatile board meetings with the care-free and rebellious Jason. But Larry loved that, because he felt that it would get the best out of everybody.

"Oh my God, I heard Sarah talking about it, I thought she was joking. You seriously want to invest in soccer?!" Jason was mocking Larry's latest idea that he pitched during their board meeting.

"Yeah, why is that a bad idea?" Larry replied.

"Soccer!! Why?" Replied Jason.

"I like soccer, I think it might be a good venture", Larry answered.

"Larry, you don't invest in something because you like it. You invest in something because its good and you can profit from it", Jason said

"I think soccer has a great potential, it can become big over here just like it is all over the world", Larry said.

"Oh please", Jason sarcastically replied.

"Hey, you are not the only one here Jason, we should get the opinion of the rest of the board", Larry told him.

"Alright, let's get their opinion. What's stupider, Larry's idea or his beard?" Jason mocking the fact that Larry had started to grow his beard.

"I agree with Larry", Coleen jumped in.

"Thank you", replied Larry, "Coleen, I'm gonna put you in charge of this, you do the research."

"I can't wait to see how that fails", Jason was still sceptical about Larry's plan.

"Whatever dude", Larry just dismissed Jason.

After the meeting, they all left to go their respective offices except for Larry and Sarah, who went to take a little tour around the office building, something that Larry insisted on doing once in a while to ensure that the employees know that the boss is always there and to keep everybody on their toes. There was another reason for this latest tour; Larry had heard that one of his newest employees was struggling to adjust. So he decided to pay him a little visit in his cubicle.

"Um, Mr. Stone! Umm...ah...how can I help you sir?" The nervous employee quickly got off his chair.

"What's your name, son?" Larry asked.

"Umm its Jim sir, Jim Barton", He replied.

"Well Jimmie, make sure you pack your stuff and go look for another job", Larry told him.

"I'm sorry sir?!" Jim was shocked.

"You're not cut out for this business, and we don't have time to babysit you until you get used to how things work here. So pack your things, you're fired!" Larry said.

Larry was ruthless. He fired Jim on the spot, in front of everyone, and left with everyone feeling sorry for the poor kid. As Jim was standing there, looking around, embarrassed at being fired, Larry and Sarah left through the hallway.

"Don't you think you were a little harsh with him? You of all people should know that there is a learning curve with this business. Don't you think he deserved a little more time?" Sarah asked him now that they were away from the other employees.

"Sweetie, don't compare him to me. I could afford to be an idiot because I had nothing to lose back then, my business was worthless. It's a multimillion dollar company now, we can't afford to have idiots working for us and bringing the company down", Larry was firm with his decision and wasn't going to be swayed by Sarah.

The board meetings kept getting more heated between Larry and Jason, which made them unbearable for the rest of the board. Jason always had a big mouth and wasn't scared to go head to head with someone at work, even if it was the boss. But Larry had changed now, he became an authoritarian figure who wanted everyone to know that he was the boss. It was a volatile cocktail which was bound to boil over at some point. But it was Sarah who would crack, and accidentally let slip a secret that the board had managed to hide from Larry ever since they started working for him. It was time for another meeting between Larry and the board, which for everyone meant another hour of Larry and Jason arguing with each other.

"Jason, I'm sick and tired of your antics! Grow up and learn who you're dealing with. I'm not 17 anymore, I'm the boss here, show some respect." Larry ordered Jason. But Jason was not scared at all, and he sarcastically lifted his hand to give a thumbs up, a move which angered Larry who kept staring at Jason with a raised eyebrow.

"Do that again!" Larry dared him, but he didn't oblige.

"No, you're right Springsteen. Here, you make the call, Jason said as he slid the folder that was in front of him towards Larry.

As they were in a heated debate, Sarah was surprisingly quiet, looking down at the floor. After Jason and Larry stopped, Susan noticed Sarah and she asked her if everything was OK.

"What's wrong? Something bothering you?" Susan asked Sarah.

"I don't like how we conduct our meetings. This is not how WE used to do it!" Sarah said, but what made that comment suspicious to Larry was that as she said that, she pointed at everyone except for Larry, as if she was referring to meetings without him, which he didn't quite understand.

Looking on curiously, Larry asked, "What do you mean? We have always done our meetings like this."

Everyone was silent. Sarah was staring at the floor, realizing that she had just made a terrible mistake.

"Sarah, honey, I'm not gonna ask again", Larry said.

"It's nothing, it's just that we used to work together before we came to work for you, and our meetings weren't as hostile as yours", Sarah finally replied. What was ironic was that Sarah was the one who told them to keep that fact a secret, because she was the one that got closest to Larry and she knew that he didn't trust people that easily. She was certain that he would get the wrong idea because he was always curious as to why they came to work for him.

"You used to work together?" Larry said with a raised eyebrow and while scratching his beard. "How come nobody mentioned this interesting fact before?"

Nobody replied, for they did not know what to say. And Sarah's skills at lying was not gonna help them now.

"So you were all friends working together and you heard about a stupid little 17-year-old who didn't know what he was doing and you thought hey, we could easily take over this guy's company and then throw him under the bus afterwards. Was that what you were thinking?" Larry asked.

"C'mon Larry, that's not what happened", Sarah replied.

"Then why did you lie to me? Why did you both lie to me?" Larry said as he pointed to Sarah and Jason. "I asked you why you came here, why didn't you say that you came together?" Larry asked, to which neither Jason nor Sarah had an answer.

"No reply, huh? Alright then, meeting dismissed", Larry said.

Larry left the meeting while everyone glared at Sarah. Larry began to recall when they all first came to work for him and how he had found it strange that 6 well-qualified individuals had come to work for him all at the same time. Now that he knew they were friends and colleagues before working for him, he started to question why they did that. What was their plan all along? Did they just take advantage of a 17-year-old kid, help him build his business so that they could force him out later? That little slip from Sarah changed the way he looked at his 5 board members, and it convinced Larry that their master plan was to eventually take over his company. Larry noticed how Sarah cracked under pressure; he thought he could get all the details from her. Their wedding day was near and Larry still wanted to go ahead despite his suspicions because he really was in love with her, and now that she will become his wife, he felt that he could easily pressure her into telling him anymore secrets that they have. A month passed by, Larry and Sarah were now married and they were ready for their honeymoon.

"You guys go enjoy yourselves. Make sure you take lots of pictures, Maldives is a beautiful place", Jason said to them.

"We will. Make sure things run smoothly while we are away. We are only gonna be gone for a couple of weeks, don't do anything stupid", Larry knew it's not the best idea to have Jason in charge, but he was the most qualified. Yet just to be safe, Larry put someone outside the company in-charge of keeping an eye on Jason.

Jason has taken charge of the day-to-day activities in the absence of both Larry and Sarah. While he was in his office, he received a visit from an old friend, a friend he hasn't seen for a few years, it was David Lawrence. David has endured the worst years of his life. The divorce ruined him financially. He had lost his job and was working part time with a salary that was not even a third of what he used to make. He was forced to leave his home and was now living in a small apartment. His contract at his job was nearing its end and he had to find a new job quickly. He began to contact his former colleagues whom he had helped out in the past, to see if they can help him get a job.

"I'll be damned! David freaking Lawrence standing in front of me! Long time no see, how have you been?" Jason got up to greet his old friend as he walked into his office.

"I'm okay, how have you been?" David asked.

"Okay, been pretty busy lately with all the work. Have a seat", Jason replied as the two men sat down.

"I came to ask you a favour. I'm in a really bad situation now, and I could use some help. I wouldn't just go around asking for help from anybody, but you owe me Jason", David told him.

"I'm sorry man, but I can't help you, I don't think we have any vacancies. Even if we did, I don't have the power to hire people. You will have to talk to Larry", Jason explained.

"Can't you talk to him for me? Recommend me", David asked.

"I wish I could, but he's away now. Plus whenever he is here, we rarely see each other at work, you know he's always busy, I'm always busy. It would be difficult to find time to talk to him", Jason said.

Jason's reaction was such that it made David feel like he didn't want to bother himself with David's problem. This made David feel sad because he had already lost his wife, his daughter, and his money. And now he felt like he had lost one of his oldest friends. Jason didn't mean to be cruel to one of his oldest friends, but he was just on a power trip; he was now a high-ranking member of a major company, and was looking down on David, and he didn't want to waste his time with his problems.

"Ok, thanks anyway", David left frustrated, not knowing what he will do now.

As David left, Jason turned back to his computer screen to get back to what he was working on.

"SHIT!" It was only after David left that he realized how badly he just treated his old friend. He banged his hand on his forehead, frustrated with himself, and wasn't able to focus on getting back to work. Jason felt guilty about how he treated David and was thinking of a way of helping him. Talking to Larry about hiring David was out of the question. Their friendship dissolved a long time ago and it was now just a volatile professional relationship. So Jason knew Larry wasn't going to do him a favour and hire his friend. Jason's phone was ringing and he picked it up to see that it was his lawyer.

"Hey Eric, what's up...yeah we are meeting this weekend...oh Jeremy is there...he didn't tell me...wait...get my papers ready too, I'm coming over now."

Jason had an idea to help David, and he quickly left his office, heading to see his lawyer who was already meeting with his brother Jeremy. What Jason had in mind would remain a secret for now, even to David. But when this secret would be revealed, it will reveal with it a conspiracy that had happened years ago, a conspiracy orchestrated by David and Jason.

"Can I get another beer please", David asked the bartender.

"Here you go", the bartender pushed a beer across the counter.

David had hit rock bottom. He was sitting in a sports bar drinking his sorrows away. There was no use in drinking responsibly anymore, for he now saw alcohol as a medicine that helped him forget the pain that he was going through.

"What's the matter there buddy?" The bartender asked.

"Is it that clear that I'm miserable?" David replied.

"Well, there is a hell of a football game on the screen behind you and instead you are facing me and drinking your 5th beer now. Having girl problems?" the bartender asked.

"I got a question for you - have you ever been so drunk that you made a terrible mistake, and you let that mistake eat you up and destroy you?" David asked.

"A drunken mistake huh? There was this one time I got drunk with my buddies and we met up with three girls, and I was so drunk that I took a picture with the three girls and sent the photo to my wife! Boy that was stupid! Was your mistake similar?" The bartender asked.

"…Yeah…it was similar", David said as he smiled. He smiled because he felt that it was hopeless talking to someone about what was hurting him.

"Man, we have all made mistakes when drunk. Don't let it get the better of you, cheer up bro. I tell you what, this last beer is on me", the bartender chuckled.

"Thanks man", David said. He finished his beer and walked back home.

Larry and Sarah returned from their honeymoon and quickly got back to work. In the middle of the day, however, Larry abruptly stopped what he was doing and left his office, and went to the parking lot without talking to anybody. Larry was sitting alone in his Bentley, when the passenger door opened and a man got in.

"Thanks for meeting me." Larry told the man.

"No problem. So what's this job you said you had for me?" The man replied.

"My parents were killed in a car accident...the police haven't done anything. There was another car involved...that caused them to crash...bring me the name of the driver."

Larry said as he gave him an envelope. The man opened it to see cash in it.

"There's more where that came from if you can get the job done. I will hire you at the company so that people won't get suspicious of seeing you around. And don't tell anyone about this."

"Alright." he said as he opened the door and got out of the car, leaving Larry with an intense stare, looking out the windshield of his car. He had finally done what he had dreamed of for so long; he hired a private investigator to solve the mystery of who caused his parents accident.

PART NINE

IN HIS HEAD

9

It was time for the monthly board meeting at JL Enterprises. Larry was already sitting at the head of the table, waiting, as one by one, the board members walked in and took their seats. Larry hadn't forgotten what happened the last time, and he was planning to deal with it. Larry feared Jason the most, since he was arrogant, stubborn and was a perfect candidate to lead a rebellion within the company. Larry waited until everyone was seated, and he remained quiet for a few minutes before he finally addressed them.

"Alright, things are gonna change now. We will conduct these meetings orderly. Nobody crosses the line, you only speak when I ask you to", Larry stamped his authority.

"Why?" Jason sarcastically responded. "Our meetings are more productive the way they have always been. Why change it?"

"Because I say so! And if you don't like it Jason, there's the door!" Larry told Jason.

"C'mon Larry, are you threatening to fire me!? This company wouldn't be what it is if it wasn't for me. You wouldn't be sitting in that chair if we hadn't come to work for you. If you want to fire me go ahead and do it, don't be shy! I would love to see what you would do without me!!" Jason was not scared of Larry's threat.

Larry leaned forward in his chair with an evil smirk on his face, "No I'm not going to fire you Jason. That would be too easy! Meeting dismissed."

The ominous words from the boss left everybody confused. Larry left with that evil smirk still on his face.

But nobody could have quite possibly imagined how evil Larry's plan was. Larry had now turned the tables. Instead of him getting information from Sarah, the board members were now asking Sarah for information on what Larry was planning, especially Jason, who was pleading with Sarah to find out what Larry meant. He decided to call her in the middle of the night to ask her what was going on with Larry.

"Did you speak to him yet? I have never seen him act the way he did, it was strange. What's going on?" Jason asked Sarah on the phone.

"Don't worry Jason, it's nothing", Sarah replied. It was a quick conversation and Sarah closed the phone. But she was sitting in bed next to Larry, who knew that it was Jason on the other end.

"What did he want?" Larry asked.

"He just called to ask about work." Sarah lied.

"It's midnight, we are about to go to sleep and he is calling to ask about work?" But Larry could see through that lie.

"OK look, this is just Jason's personality; he is always troublesome and our former boss had problems with him too but he is important to us, so can't you just let it go?" It seemed that Sarah can't complete a sentence without including a lie in it. Their former boss never had any problems with Jason, she just said that to feed the idea that Larry had now built in his head, that Jason was troublesome.

"Alright, whatever you say." Larry reached over to the nightstand and got his phone. He got out of bed and went outside the room to make a call.

"Larry?" the person on the phone answered.

"I got a job for you", said Larry.

"Who is it this time?"...

"Jason Kay. Make sure you take care of it by the end of the week", Larry said.

"I can do it sooner", said Larry's personal bodyguard.

That was Larry's secret. That was how he had dealt with the rich businessman who had wanted to rival them. The 5 board members were his core team that had helped him build his empire. But nobody knew about the team that Larry had assembled to protect his empire. They consisted of just 2 people, the bodyguard, and a private investigator. Larry had a personal connection with the bodyguard. It was none other than Mark Nichols, the eldest son of Steve and Judy, his parents' friends. He knew Larry since he was young, and looked after him like a big brother ever since the day he had seen Larry sitting in the police station, badly beaten.

Everyone went to work the next day but Jason did not show up. Despite the fact that Larry and Jason became close friends, and Jason helped oversee the rise of Larry's business more than anyone else involved. Those hangouts at Jason's beach house, and countless meetings outside of work weren't enough to prevent Larry from taking the decision to eliminate what he saw as a threat to his position as the leader. No one wanted to believe that Larry had done something to him. A week passed and there was still no sign of Jason. Their last board meeting ended prematurely, so Larry ordered them to reschedule for the following week. Again, the board assembled in the meeting room waiting for Larry to come and acknowledge the disappearance of Jason. Larry walked in; he still hadn't taken his seat. He put his hands on the table and eyed each one of them.

"...As I was saying, things are gonna change now in our meetings!" As if he had just swatted a bothersome fly, Larry made no mention of Jason and he just went on with business like nothing had happened.

"But honey..." Sarah tried to intervene but was cut short by Larry.

"It's Mr. Stone! When we are in this office, I'm not your husband and you are not my wife. You are just an employee and I'm the boss! Don't you forget that! And that goes for all of you", Larry said.

After that meeting, they all went to their separate offices to continue their work. Sarah was in her office when her assistant came rushing in.

"Sorry to disturb you boss, but the police just found Jason's body. He's dead! They are saying it was a drug overdose", her assistant told her. Sarah just got confirmation of what she had already suspected.

"When did they find the body?" Sarah asked.

"This morning", her assistant replied.

Sarah felt sad as Jason was one of her oldest friends. She asked her assistant to go away and she called Jason's brother, Jeremy, to offer her condolences. He told her when the funeral was going to be, and to her surprise, Larry wanted to attend the funeral of the man he had killed. It wasn't out of his good heart, but because he didn't want people talking about why he hadn't shown up. David also heard about the news of Jason's death and wanted to pay his respects. But he didn't want anyone to recognize him there, so he went in disguise, wearing a baseball cap and over-sized sunglasses.

Everyone was seated in church, listening to Jason's brother deliver his eulogy, when Sarah looked around at the people and recognized David, sitting on the last pew. The service ended and Jason Kay was buried. David wanted to leave quickly; he put his head down and walked away only to see Sarah standing in front of him, blocking his path.

"I thought I would see you here. What happened to you? You disappeared." It had been a few years since the two had last seen each other.

"…Sarah…I could talk all day about what happened to me, but I don't feel comfortable talking here. Can we meet tomorrow?" David didn't feel comfortable talking because that Larry was chatting with other mourners just a few feet away from him.

"Sure, we can meet tomorrow", Sarah said.

Everyone quickly moved on after Jason's funeral, and things were tense now at work, with everyone fearing Larry more. His show of strength in taking out Jason worked, as far as Larry is concerned. But Larry is not an evil man, despite what he just did. It was just his failure to easily trust people that made him eliminate a threat to his position. Larry only trusted a handful of people; the Nichols and Sarah. Larry remained close to Mark, who was now his bodyguard, but he was close with Mark's parents before him. Steve and Judy stood by Larry when he lost his parents, and he never forgot that. Larry didn't just hold grudges; he also held a special place in his heart for those that were good to him. Steve's birthday was coming up, and Larry, now a millionaire, was planning something special for Steve. He called him up and told him that he would drop by after work.

"I have a surprise for you!" Larry told him.

"Oh son, at my age, surprises are not good, what are you planning?" Steve said.

"Don't worry, it's good. Both of you get dressed, me and Sarah will come pick you up", Larry said to Steve. As they all got in the car, they made a short drive which led them to a big house in the same neighbourhood where Larry's mansion was. They all got out of the car, and went inside the big house.

"Wow, your mansion wasn't big enough that you had to buy this house also?" Steve asked. Larry came towards Steve and reached out to grab his arm. He extended it and opened his palms and laid the keys to the house in his hand.

"What?! Seriously?" Replied a shocked Steve.

"It's yours! Happy birthday!!" Larry exclaimed.

"Larry, this is too much! I don't know what to say," Steve said.

"You don't have to say anything. You know I have always looked at you as a father figure since I lost my dad, and this is the least I can do for you. I just wanted to show you how much you mean to me, both of you", Larry said softly.

As Sarah went to show Judy around their new home, Larry was left alone with Steve and he saw this as the perfect time to ask about Mark.

"Where is Mark? He is not answering his phone", Larry asked.

"Oh he went off on one of his disappearing acts again", Steve said.

"Disappearing acts?" Asked a confused Larry.

"Yeah he just disappears from time to time without telling us, and then just reappears out of nowhere. Sometimes he disappears for a couple of weeks, months and once he even disappeared for a whole year. He calls it his extra dice", Steve explained.

Larry had no idea what he was talking about, so he waited until Mark showed up again to understand what he meant. Nevertheless, Steve and Judy were overwhelmed by this gift from Larry. And the timing of it exemplified who Larry is; he had just killed someone who was close to him for a few years, but someone he never trusted. Trust and loyalty were important factors in Larry's relationships. And Jason was someone he never trusted, which is why things ended the way they did for him. On the other hand, no one has ever been more loyal and trustworthy in Larry's eyes than Steve, Judy and their son Mark, and Larry never forgot that, just like he never forgot about the person that killed his parents. The idea of retribution entered his head when he was 17, and after years of wanting to know who killed his parents, it was now time for him to come face-to-face with that man.

PART TEN

AND THEN THEY MEET

10

"Hello, Richard? It's David Lawrence, how are you?"

"Hey Dave, how have you been cousin? I'm doing pretty good."

"I'm okay, how's the business going?"

"It could be better."

"Do you have any job openings?"

"Actually we could use some additions to the workforce. Work is really piling up lately. You have a friend you can recommend?"

"No actually, I was asking for me. I was wondering if I could come work for you."

"Really? Dave I think you are over-qualified for this, plus the pay is not that good to be honest with you."

"I'm at the point where I don't really care about the work or salary, as long as I'm doing something."

"Wow, I'm sorry to hear that your situation is that bad. Dave, I would be more than happy if you come work for me. When can you start?"

"Could you just give me some time to organize my things because I have lived my whole life in New York, so it might take me a couple of weeks to pick up my life and move to another place."

"Absolutely, I totally understand you. Hey, take all the time you need, just inform me a couple of days before you come so that we can get everything sorted."

David was clearing up his things, ready to move to Florida and hopefully kick-start his life again. But his heart wasn't set on leaving New York, and he wasn't really excited about the job, but he thought that it was his only choice now. However, he wanted to try his luck in New York one last time. Sarah cancelled their meeting that they agreed upon on at Jason's funeral, and she never rescheduled it for another time. David contacted her to see if she was free to meet him now. He wanted to try one last time to see if he could get a job with them. They spoke on the phone and she arranged to have lunch with him so that they could talk about his current situation.

"I got nothing left...Jennifer left me and she took Bonnie...I have no money...no job. Things haven't been the same since that night..." David began pouring his heart out to Sarah.

"You did this to yourself David! You should have listened to me. You are the smartest person I have ever met, you should have started your own business when you had the chance. You could have created something even bigger than JL Enterprises." Sarah was upset with David because she didn't like seeing him in the state that he was in. David also felt ashamed that Sarah was seeing him like this.

"I still haven't gotten over it...I keep reliving that night over and over in my head..." David then leaned forward to make sure no one in the nearby tables can hear what he was about to say next. "I killed Larry's parents! How can I move on from that??"

"You have done enough. You have to move on now and focus on yourself. Look, do you want me to talk to Larry? I will personally recommend you to work with us", Sarah said.

Sarah gave him time to think while she went to use the restroom. David took a deep breath and thought long and hard about Sarah's offer. Was David strong enough to face Larry after what he had put him through? It has been over 10 years now since the day that David killed Larry's parents in a car accident. David had nothing to lose now, and when Sarah returned to the table he agreed to meet Larry.

The next day, David went to JL Enterprises so that he can be interviewed by Larry. He was made to wait outside Larry's office for half an hour. David was looking at the clock hanging on the wall and his heartbeat became synchronized with each tick of the second-hand. Even though he was nervous, counting each second as it went by made him relax. After that long wait, the door was opened and David Lawrence and Larry Stone met for the first time.

"Mr. Stone, I'm David Lawrence. Sarah recommended me for the job opening that you have", David immediately got off his chair and introduced himself.

"Ah yes David, it's good to meet you. Come in", Larry said.

Larry invited David in his office so that he could be interviewed. As David walked in, he was amazed at how large his office was and it made David feel proud. Larry noticed that David was looking around at his office and smiling.

"What? Why are you smiling?" Larry asked.

"It's just that you have such a huge office, it must have taken years of hard work to be able to sit in an office this big", replied David.

"You have no idea!" Larry exclaimed. David didn't say anything, he just smiled.

"Now, I don't usually interview potential employees, but I was really impressed by your resume and by what Sarah told me about you, I felt like I should interview you personally", Larry told him.

Larry and David hit it off, making the interview seem as though it was just a couple of guys hanging out and talking. They talked about business, personal lives and even about sports.

"It says in your resume that you speak Spanish, that's interesting," Larry said.

"Yeah I had an internship in Barcelona when I was in college, can't say that I'm fluent, but I am certainly above average", David replied.

"Barcelona! That's nice! Have you been to any soccer games while you were there?" Larry asked.

"Yeah living in Spain, you can't help but get caught up in soccer fever", replied David.

"You know, I am really interested in opening an office overseas, and Barcelona is one of our options. You think heading the team there is something that will interest you?" Larry asked.

"Si!" David replied.

David felt really comfortable about the way that the interview was going; he was worried that it would have been awkward for him to be in the same room as Larry.

"You know, I never thought I would enjoy interviewing somebody. You seem like a great guy David. I can see why Sarah has been friends with you for so many years. Since I'm the boss here, I can give you an immediate reply and tell you that you will definitely be working with us. We just need to sort out the formalities and we will probably have a contract ready by next week. It is gonna have a pretty good salary, so don't worry about your financial situation anymore", Larry said winking at David.

"Thank you sir, I can't wait to work for you", replied a happy David.

The whole meeting couldn't have been anymore perfect for David, and he left the office very happy. After David

left, Larry called his private investigator because he had
a new job for him.

"Hey, are there any new developments, or are
you still at a dead end?" Larry said.

"No sir, nothing new", replied his private
investigator.

"Well I got another job for you. I want you to do
a background check on an individual. His name is David
Lawrence. He's gonna be working for me so I gotta
make sure he's an honest guy", Larry said.

After Larry found out that his board members lied to
him about working with each other before they came to
work for him, he had become suspicious about
everybody and from that very moment, he had decided
that anybody wanting to work for him had to go through
a background check. It was ironic because the reason
Larry hired the private investigator all those years ago
was to investigate his parents' accident. And now,
without knowing, Larry just ordered a background check
on the man responsible for the accident.

Larry enjoyed David's company so much that he thought
it would be a good idea to hang out in an informal
setting with Sarah.

"What do you think about having dinner with
David some time?" Larry asked Sarah. "I am thinking of

offering him the role that Jason had. A guy with a mind like David's can take this company even higher."

"I told you! He's not only smart but he's a good guy as well so you won't have the same problems with him as you had with Jason", Sarah replied, "I will call him to see if he's free this weekend."

Sarah called David and he didn't mind having dinner with them. Since his first meeting with Larry went really well, David was at ease about being in the same room as him. They all agreed to have dinner at a new restaurant that had just opened in the city.

"I'm looking for a table under the name of Larry Stone", David informed the hostess.

"You must be Mr. Lawrence. Mr. Stone and his wife are already at the table, if you would please follow me", the hostess led David to the table.

"Good to see you again Dave", Larry said.

"Good to see you too sir, Sarah", David replied.

"Sir? I'm not your boss yet, you can call me Larry." After the greetings, the three sat down to enjoy the night.

"It took you a while to get here, did you get lost?" Larry asked.

"No actually I took the subway, I don't drive", David replied.

"How come?" Larry asked.

"…It's just cheaper to take the subway." David was flustered by that question, because he has never driven since the night he accidentally killed Larry's parents.

"I don't drive either, I don't like it. That's why I have a personal chauffeur. I just have a Bentley that I like to drive around in just to listen to music and clear my head. It was my dad's favourite car, he always dreamed of owning one but…that never happened", Larry responded. "So you two know each other a long time huh?" Larry asked.

"Yeah I was friends with his ex-wife, remember honey I asked him to come work for us before", Sarah said. But this was of course a lie that she was friends with David's ex-wife, and David knew that but he didn't say anything.

"Yeah I remember, why did you turn down that offer before?" Larry asked David.

"I was going through a tough time with my divorce, if I had come back then with the state of mind that I was in, I wouldn't have been much help to you guys", David said.

"I understand that. It seems like it was meant to be that you come work with us though, because here we are years after you turned down Sarah's offer and you are about to be our newest employee. Here's to a successful partnership, cheers!" Larry said as the three of them raised their glasses.

"Honey, David is a fan of soccer like you. Larry made an offer to buy a franchise in the MLS", Sarah said.

"Yeah, we talked about it during the interview", Larry said.

While they were enjoying their night, an old face showed up at the restaurant with his family. Scott Sheppard, the man who quit on Sarah and Larry when they were struggling.

"Hey! What a coincidence, it's good to see you guys, how are you doing?" Scott greeted them.

"We're doing great, how have you been?" Sarah replied.

"I'm good. It's great to see what you have done with the business. I never imagined that it would become this big. Great job Larry!" Scott said as he extended his arm to shake hands with Larry.

Larry however has been quiet since he saw Scott. And he still hadn't extended his hand to shake Scott's.

"You got some nerve showing up in this restaurant. Don't you know that I own this place?" Larry said.

"What? You can't still be angry about me quitting are you?" Scott asked.

"Angry? You quit because you doubted me! You didn't believe that I was good enough to lead the business. Yeah, Sarah told me what you thought about me", Larry told Scott.

"I'm sorry, I didn't think that the business had potential but obviously I was wrong", Scott replied.

"No, you didn't think that I had potential! Now, if you would, please leave with your family and go somewhere else", Larry said.

"What? Look, I'm sorry I doubted you okay. I'm just here to have dinner with my family", Scott said.

"No, you didn't believe in me and my business, I don't think that you should enjoy the fruits of my success." Larry explained. "Could you please escort this man and his family out of my restaurant", Larry said to a large suited man who was sitting at a nearby table.

"This is ridiculous! Sarah, do something!" Scott was embarrassed to be grabbed by his arm and led outside in front of his family. Sarah however, was quiet.

"So long Scott, and I will be sure to ban you from ever entering anything that I own." Larry said as he waved goodbye to him.

Larry again showed that if you treat him badly, he will not forget it. Scott was escorted out and Larry sat back down.

"Can you believe that guy?!" Larry said to Sarah. "It's funny we were just talking about it, Dave, that guy was with us when we were still struggling, and he quit! He was the guy you were supposed to replace the first time. He didn't have faith in the business or me, and now he just walks in my restaurant expecting me to forget that anything ever happened. What an idiot!" Larry informed David of the history between him and Scott. But David already knew that. Scott was a former colleague of his but he didn't want Larry to know that.

That whole incident certainly soured the rest of the night. Especially from David's standpoint, who was silent during the argument. He again began feeling uneasy about being with Larry, because he saw that Larry held a grudge on a man that quit and made him feel bad. He figured he must also still be holding a grudge on the man who killed his parents. After they finished dinner, Larry insisted that they go back to his mansion and David can borrow a car from his collection to drive back.

"I got a few cars to choose from, borrow it for now and you can bring it back when we have your contract ready and you can get your official company car", Larry told David.

"No, I don't know about borrowing one of your cars", David said.

"I told you, I don't like to drive, it's okay. If you are worried about damaging the car, then don't. I have enough money to buy another one, so go ahead and scratch the hell out of it if you want", Larry joked.

Larry was not the kind of guy who takes no for an answer. He told David to borrow one of his cars, and there was nothing that David could have said to change Larry's mind. The three of them arrived back to Larry's mansion, where Larry again insisted that David stay and have coffee before leaving. Sarah went to make the coffee while Larry and David waited for her and for the chauffer to bring the keys so that David could choose a car to borrow.

"Wow, you have an amazing house. It looks even bigger on the inside. Of course I couldn't help but notice that", David said as he pointed to a Manchester United banner hanging on the wall.

"I had to have that! If it wasn't for Sarah, I would've had one in every room of the house." Larry joked.

Sarah came back with the coffee and soon after the chauffer arrived with the car keys.

"Sir, here are the cars that are available", the chauffer said as he laid the keys on the table.

"Let's see what's available. You have the Audi R8, Range Rover and the Bentley?" Larry looked at his chauffer. "Nobody uses the Bentley but me. I said bring the keys for the other cars!"

"I'm sorry sir", the chauffer took the keys to the Bentley off the table.

"So, which one do you want?" Larry asked David to choose.

"I'll take the Range Rover", David said.

"Good choice, enjoy it", Larry said.

David took the keys and finished his coffee and was ready to get going.

"Thank you guys for a lovely evening and for inviting me into your home I really enjoyed this night. And thanks again for the car Larry", David said

"Don't mention it. Hey, you know what's next month right? El Clasico! You gotta come watch it here in my home cinema", Larry said

"Ugh! I hate when he has game night. I always tell him to inform me beforehand when he will arrange it so that I can get out of the house", Sarah said

"Sure thing, save me a seat", David said, "I see you still haven't turned Sarah into a soccer fan."

"And he never will!" Sarah said.

"Man, I stopped trying a long time ago. She's too stubborn to even watch one game", Larry joked.

Larry and David shared a laugh at Sarah's expense. It turned out to be a good night for David. It seemed that it could have been be a bad night after the confrontation between Scott and Larry. But it didn't, and it certainly ended on a high note as well with Larry giving him one of his cars. But this eventful night had one last unexpected turn. After David said goodbye to them, he turned towards the door and was making his way out when he noticed a framed photo of Larry with his parents, set on the table. He stopped and stared at the photo, and Larry noticed him.

"Those are my parents. They were killed when I was 17", Larry explained.

"I'm sorry to hear that", replied David

"Yeah, they were the best parents anyone could have asked for…" Larry began biting his lips in anger, and his eyebrows became furrowed.

"It seems that you are still upset about their loss?" David asked.

"Wouldn't you be?! They were all I had and they were taken away from me by some idiot. The worst part was that the guy didn't even get punished for what he did. He fled the scene of the accident and the police didn't even try to look for him. I tell you, put me in a room alone with that guy and he wouldn't get out alive!!" Little did Larry know that he was in a room with the guy who killed his parents. But there was something about the photo that had David perplexed. In the photo, they were all smiling, and Larry was holding a sign that said it's a girl, as Jack was pointing at Lindsey's belly.

"You have a younger sister?" David asked. "I didn't know that."

"Yeah my mom was 3 months pregnant in that picture…but they were killed a couple of days after taking this picture. That's why I had this picture framed, it was the last picture we ever took together", Larry explained.

David just received the shock of his life; he never knew that Lindsey was pregnant. He already thought that what he had done was horrible. And he never thought that it could get worse, but it just did. The vivid images of that tragic night just came screaming back to him. The sight of Jack and Lindsey, motionless in their car, was an image he managed to subdue the whole time he was with Larry. But now knowing that it wasn't just two people that he killed that night, it made that image appear even more horrifying. David hadn't just killed Larry's parents, he also killed his unborn sister. David killed Larry's whole family.

"I'm...I'm sorry for your loss." David said as he hurriedly made his way out. He couldn't even make eye contact with Larry let alone be in the same room as him. David was thinking that there was no way he could work for Larry now. He managed to suppress all the guilt that he had for killing Larry's parents, and finally, after so many years, he had the courage to face Larry. But knowing that he killed his sister as well made all that guilt come back, like an avalanche, and David was now buried under his guilt again. David was disappointed, because he had to look for another job now, because he couldn't face Larry again. Larry, on the other hand, was excited to be adding David to the company, not only because he could see that he was a smart man, but Larry also felt that they could become good friends. It had always been an issue that Larry struggled with; he never made friends easily and he would try too hard when meeting someone to try to make them like him. Jason might have been considered a close friend, but Larry felt that the friendship was spurred on by sympathy that Jason had towards Larry, and not because he liked him. Larry always saw his dad as his only guy friend, and what he saw in David reminded him of his dad. It wasn't strange for David. He always had a certain charm and charisma about him that made people feel very comfortable around him. Even when he was down on his luck and depressed, Larry could still see that charm in David. Unfortunately, that friendship would never flourish, because the next time the two would meet, David Lawrence would end up dead at the hands of Larry Stone.

David's contract was ready, and Larry wanted to personally call him to congratulate him. He called David but he wasn't answering, Sarah then walked into Larry's office.

"Have you spoken to David today? I am trying to call him to tell him that his contract is ready but he's not answering", Larry told Sarah.

"Yeah, about that, I spoke with him yesterday and he said thanks but he was going to decline the job offer", Sarah replied.

"Decline?! Did he find another job?" Larry asked.

"No, he didn't really give me a reason. The chauffer already went to take back the car from him", Sarah said.

"That's strange, why would a guy in desperate need of money decline this job? He seemed excited to come work here when I interviewed him. If you talk to him again tell him to call me. If he's gonna decline then he should at least be a man about it and give me the reason why", Larry angrily threw the contract in the trash. Larry waited for that call from David but it would never come. Later that day, Larry's private investigator came in having just finished the background check on David Lawrence.

"I have the background check that you wanted", said the P.I.

"That's OK, you can just throw it in the trash on top of his contract, he's not gonna be working here anymore", Larry said.

"I still think you should look at what I found", insisted the private investigator.

Larry took the papers and was stunned to see that David wasn't just an old friend of Sarah, he was her old colleague, he was a former colleague of all the board members, working together in the same company before coming to work for Larry. It was something that David conveniently forgot to add in the resume he gave to Larry.

"He was with them?! I don't get this, it can't be a coincidence that they all worked together and that they all came at the same time to work for me. And now David was also with them! Why didn't he come from the beginning with all of them?" Larry was getting angered by the secret of them working together and not telling him. And he was about to get a little more angry.

"I also did a check of his criminal record. It was clean, just a couple of traffic violations. But I think you are going to find this particular traffic violation very interesting", the private investigator handed Larry the paper.

Larry couldn't believe it, his eyes were wide open staring at the paper. He got up off his chair with the paper still in his hand and a tear rolling down his cheek. He still hasn't said a word. The private investigator was looking at Larry and smiling.

"We got him", He said to Larry.

Larry wiped the tear from his face and proceeded to get a large envelope from his desk drawer. It was filled with money, and he gave it to the private investigator. Larry then threw the paper on his desk and left his office still without saying a single word. As he was leaving, he bumped into Sarah.

"Mr. Stone…" Sarah tried to get his attention but he just ignored her.

The private investigator left soon after with the envelope in his hand and a big smile on his face.

"Well, my job here is done. Have a good day ma'am", he said to Sarah.

Sarah was confused, she felt something was wrong and she went into Larry's office to find the papers on his desk. "Oh my God!" was her only response when she looked at the papers. She immediately pulled out her phone to send a message to David.

"He knows!"

It was just two words, but they would signal the end for David Lawrence.

PART ELEVEN

RETRIBUTION

11

Larry Stone now knows that David Lawrence was the man responsible for the death of his parents. After storming out of his office, he needed to be alone. He got in his car and told his driver to take him back home. But when he arrived, he didn't go inside, instead, he asked his driver to bring the keys to his Bentley.

After ordering the driver to go away, Larry got in the car and sat in the driver's seat for a few minutes, still trying to comprehend the information that he had just received. He had given up hope of ever finding the man responsible for his parents' death after his private investigator told him that he hit a dead end. Larry began to cry, exactly like he had cried as a 17-year-old kid lying on the floor after hearing the news about his parents' death; he had never gotten off the floor. Larry took out his phone and was going to call his bodyguard to give him the order that he has been waiting years to give, but he couldn't. He shut off his phone and opened the locked glove compartment for which he only had the key to, and he took out a Desert Eagle, the same gun that once belonged to his dad. He loaded the gun with just one bullet. It was the same bullet that Larry had loaded many years ago when he wanted to take his own life. He saved that particular bullet as a reminder of how low he got. Larry will now use this bullet on the man who made him think about killing himself, the man who took away the two most valuable things in Larry's life.

David has just seen the message that Sarah sent him. The first thought to cross his mind was that he had to get away from the city. He had to forget about looking for another job and getting his life together. He knew that if Larry found him, he would kill him. David wanted to call his cousin in Florida to book him a ticket as soon as possible; he thought he would be his only escape from the situation that he is in. But he couldn't call him. At that moment, Sarah was calling David. He didn't answer the phone; he let it ring until it stopped. David has been running away from facing Larry for years. He was tired of running away, and it was time for him to face his fate. He shut off his phone as well and decided to face Larry in the hopes that he could convince him to forgive him.

David left the door to his apartment ajar and sat on his chair waiting for Larry to show up. It was only a few minutes later that Larry would be standing in the doorway. The two men stared at each other with differing emotions on their faces. Larry had the look of anger and sadness; the look of a man that came to do one thing and wasn't gonna be stopped. David on the other hand, had the look of fear similar to a child that had done something wrong and was about to be punished. Larry walked in the apartment and locked the door behind him as David got off his chair.

"How did you know? Did Sarah tell you?" David asked.

"You wanna know how I found out?" Larry replied. "I was looking at your record. You have a few traffic violations, but only one of them is a speeding violation; 27th of March 2004, at 11:27pm, Shore Parkway! Your whole life, you just have a single speeding violation, and it was the same day, the same location and the same time that my parents were killed. It seems like you were trying to run away from something that night. Am I right?" Larry asked him.

"You are right, I was running away from the crash, I should have helped them…I was scared, I drank a lot that night and it would have ruined my life if I had waited till the police showed up", David replied. Perhaps the emotional charge that was present at that moment messed with David's mind, because although he did speed off, he never did get a speeding violation that night.

David couldn't hold back his tears any longer. "I'm sorry."

Larry reached back and pulled out his gun ready to kill David.

"NO WAIT! PLEASE GIVE ME A CHANCE TO EXPALIN EVERYTHING TO YOU!" David said.

"Give you a chance? You had plenty of chances to right what you did wrong. You could have helped my parents, but you didn't. You could have come over with your buddies when they came to work for me, and I might have forgiven you then. Maybe I am too arrogant to admit this to them but I will always be indebted to them. Even though they turned out to be a bunch of lying, manipulative people, they did help me build my business, and they also stood by me when I needed someone by my side. You could have come over with them, but you didn't. You even had a chance when you were in my home, LOOKING AT A PICTURE OF MY PARENTS; THE PEOPLE THAT YOU KILLED! YOU

COULD HAVE SAID SOMETHING.
BUT...YOU...DIDN'T! The way I see it Dave, you are a coward. You had your chances...you don't deserve another..." Larry said.

"I HELPED YOU..." David screamed out.

'BANG...'

Larry pulled the trigger, and with that one bullet, ended David Lawrence's life. After David's body dropped to the floor, Larry didn't run away. He dropped the gun on the floor and just sat on the chair. Looking at David's lifeless body that was laying in a pool of blood, Larry tried to remember his parents' faces. His journey to avenge them took many years, and as far as he was feeling at that specific moment, Larry was satisfied, he finally had closure, and his parents could rest knowing that the person that killed them had received the punishment he deserved. The sound of the gunshot had not gone unnoticed, and the police had arrived at the scene. As they barged into the apartment, they saw the body on the floor and Larry sitting on the chair. With their guns aimed at Larry, they ordered him to stand up and put his hands on his head. With ice running through his veins now, Larry calmly stood up and put his hands behind his head and turned around, giving his back to the officers so that they could handcuff him. But were his actions justified? Did he really kill the man solely responsible for his parent's death? What would happen now? The death of David Lawrence was inevitable, but his death will unravel what has really been going on for so many years. If it was fate that finally brought David and Larry face to face, then in this instance, fate had a name.

(News headline)

Millionaire Larry Stone Arrested For First-Degree Murder, Trial to Begin Next Week

David Lawrence always wanted to confess what he did to Larry Stone. But he never had the courage to face him. And when he did, Larry didn't give him a chance. So David wanted to make sure that Larry would somehow learn the truth, even if it was after David died. David met his lawyer a few years before he even met Larry, to discuss the contents of his will.

(News coverage, two journalists discussing)

"Larry Stone, as we all know, is a very well established man who has come a long way into building what is now an empire. David Lawrence, on the other hand, is a nobody. He's in his 40's, unemployed, divorced. So the question on everyone's mind is why? Why would Larry Stone risk everything he has worked for to kill David Lawrence?"

With Larry Stone's trial in full effect, his company's stock had taken a major hit. Sarah had now taken temporary control.

(Reporter outside courtroom)

"Everyone is anticipating to hear what's written in Mr. Lawrence's will, because according to his lawyer. David Lawrence's will is the key to this whole case, and it will answer all of our questions and will finally put this case that has rocked the country, to bed."

David's lawyer handed the will to the judge to prove its authenticity. The judge verified it and handed the will back to the lawyer so that he could read it out.

"I David Lawrence, don't have valuable possessions to distribute. All I ask is this will finds Mr. Larry Stone. I have a confession to make to Mr. Stone. It is something that I never told anyone about, not even my wife. On the 27th of March 2004, my office had a party to celebrate our latest achievement. I made the mistake of drinking too much, something that I don't usually do. The party lasted all night, and I thought that I would be able to drive back home in the state that I was in. I just had to drop off my friend and go back home, which was a very short distance. As I was driving though, I lost focus and veered into the opposite lane, causing the oncoming car to swerve away from me and crash into a tree. The people in that car were Jack and Lindsey Stone. I was struggling with myself trying to decide whether I should go help them or not. I knew that if I stayed until the police showed up, I would be in trouble. I looked over at the wrecked car, and I saw Jack with little life left in him staring back at me. We stared at each other for a few seconds before he finally passed away. I will never forget that moment for as long as I live; there lay a man and his wife who were in a situation where they desperately needed help, and I was the man responsible. But what made it worse was that I just sat there and watched them die. Me not doing anything was the last thing that Jack Stone saw, and I was never able to forgive myself for that. I later found out that they had a son, Larry, and that he was left alone to take care of his father's business. I kept track of him to see how he was doing, he was in a mess. It killed me to see what I had put him through. I wanted to help him, but I wasn't strong enough to go and face him. I asked my close colleagues to do me a favour, I lied to them and told them that Jack and Lindsey were old friends and if they could go help Larry get through this tough time, but he mustn't know that I sent them. They agreed to do it if I promised to be in charge of the business. They always wanted me to start my own business and I agreed to their demands to lead the business from afar. We would meet twice a week to discuss Larry's business and how to improve it. Even though I lost all my money from this and my divorce, it makes me feel proud to see how far Larry has taken his business. And I just hope that by doing this for him, he could find it in his heart to one day forgive me."

The people in the courtroom started to whisper to each other. Is it true what they just heard? Larry was seeking revenge and David was the real brains behind JL Enterprises? Some people in the courtroom had a complete change in their views about this case. Those who thought Larry was this evil tyrant actually began to sympathize with him. They thought that it was Larry's right to kill the man who killed his parents. While others felt sincerity in David's will, and that there was no malice from David's standpoint, that the events of that night were just an awful accident and that Larry should have forgiven him.

"Order in the courtroom!" The judge quieted them.

"In light of recent developments, we now know that you did in fact kill the man responsible for your parents death, and while people might applaud you for doing that, I personally don't agree in taking the law into your own hands and punishing people as you see fit. We also now know that David helped you build your wealth, I assume that this is the first time you know about this", the judge addressed Larry.

"Yes your honour", Larry replied.

"Then I have to ask you Mr. Stone, was it worth it? You did kill the man responsible for your parent's death, but you also killed the man responsible for building your empire." The judge asked Larry.

Larry took a few seconds to respond. He stood up, lifted his head and looked the judge straight in the eye.

"Your honour, I should have been with them that night. They wanted me to come with them but I told them no. You don't know for how long I kept the thought in my head of what would have happened if I was with them. Could I have saved them, or would I have died with them? And you ask me about my empire? I don't care about my empire! My empire is worth 500 million dollars. I own businesses all across the country. I have homes in L.A and New York. Do you think that I'm satisfied? No, I'm not satisfied. Not because I want more, but because my parents never got to see what I have become! I always put pressure on myself as their only child to make them proud. And I can't tell you how many times I let my dad down, but he would always push me and encourage me. Okay, David helped build my empire, but so did his friends that he sent to work for me...." Larry suddenly realized something and he stopped talking.

"Mr. Stone, is there anything else that you would like to add?" The judge asked Larry.

"...No...no your honour", Larry sat back down with a puzzled look on his face.

Larry just remembered what David said in his will about dropping off a friend the night of the accident. He also remembered what David said to him when he confronted him in his apartment.

("How did you know? Did Sarah tell you?")

Sarah knew about the accident even though David stated in his will that he never told anyone about it. Larry slowly turned his head around and looked at Sarah sitting in the courtroom with one thought in his head.

("*She was with him!!*")

PART TWELVE

THE DAY IT ALL CHANGED

12

Saturday, March 27th 2004, David Lawrence was on his way to a party organized by his colleagues. He also happened to be driving Sarah to the party with him since her scheduled lift had cancelled at the last minute.

"So how's everything with you?" Sarah asked David while they were on their way to the party.

"Can't complain, things are good", David replied.

"Then why were you looking at apartments in Florida? Are you moving?" Sarah asked.

"Hmm, no I don't think so. I had a job interview last week so I was looking at real estate in Florida, but having thought about it more, I'm gonna decline the offer if they do offer me the job. And, how did you know I was looking at apartments?" David asked.

"I'm eagle eyed!" Sarah joked. "Oh yeah, I saw Bonnie the other day, she's really cute", Sarah said.

"Yeah Jennifer told me, yeah she is", David replied.

"Are you gonna groom her to be like you? Career-wise I mean", Sarah asked.

"No, I'm not gonna force her to be something she is not. I will encourage her to pursue whatever she wants", David replied.

David and Sarah arrived at the party, and David pretended to be surprised that he was the guest of honour, as Sarah had let the cat out of the bag on their drive there. But it didn't make a difference to the ever humble David, who was enjoying the party with his colleagues.

"Where is Jennifer? Why didn't she come?" David's boss asked.

"She had plans with her friends", replied David.

"She doesn't like me", Sarah interrupted, "That's why she didn't come, right?"

"Well...um", David struggled to respond.

"It's OK, most women don't like me. I think they feel intimidated by me, that's why", Sarah wasn't bothered by it.

Jason Kay, being the host of the party, was going around the place and making sure that everybody was enjoying themselves. He came over to David and offered him another drink.

"Oh no, no, I had my one beer already. That's it for me", David refused the offer.

"Dude what the hell, why are you such a baby?! I never met anybody who drinks just one beer and calls it a day", Jason responded.

"What's going on?" David's boss asked.

"Sir, could you tell David that he has to get drunk or else you will fire him", Jason said.

"Dave, don't listen to JK. You just bought in 1.3 million dollars into the company, you can drink as little or as much as you want", the boss told David. He liked to joke around with his employees, especially with Jason, who pretended to laugh at his boss' joke.

"I know how to get him to drink", Sarah said with a smile on her face.

"Is that my phone?" David said while checking his pockets.

Sarah had taken David's phone. "Yup, and I have my fingers ready to call your wife and tell her that you kissed me!" Sarah threatened.

"What? I didn't kiss you", David responded.

"Yeah but she doesn't know that it's a lie", Sarah said.

"Oh she got you", Jason chimed.

Sarah was just about to dial before David stopped her.

"Alright fine, I will drink! You guys are evil I swear!" David succumbed to their pressure.

Sarah gave him back his phone and David drank some more. David caving in to their pressure ended up being a good thing for the party, as it turned out to be a wild and fun night. But, it would have a tragic ending. David ended up drinking a lot, and it was getting late. He decided it was best to get going because he still had to drop off Sarah.

"Thanks guys for the great gesture and having this party in my honour, but we have to get going now", David said as he stumbled towards the door.

"Whoa, are you sure you can drive there Dave?" His boss asked with concern.

"Yeah I will be fine. Which reminds me, if I see you tomorrow Jason, I am gonna kill you", David jokingly threatened.

"Tomorrow is Sunday, we don't have work, so you will have to wait", Jason joked. "And why are you only blaming me? Sarah got you to drink too." Jason pointed out.

"Fine, I will kill Sarah tonight, and I will wait and kill you on Monday!" David said as everybody laughed. It was a cruel irony that David was joking about killing; little did he know that he would actually kill people that night.

The two said goodbye and left, wanting to get back home and straight to bed because they were both exhausted from the party. The exhaustion and the effects of the alcohol were clear on David as he was not driving well and kept swerving into the opposite lane.

"Are you okay?" Sarah asked.

"Now you see why I don't like to drink a lot. I'm okay", David replied.

Because it was late at night, there weren't many cars on the road. There was just one car approaching in the opposite direction. It was a Ford Taurus, and in it were Jack and Lindsey Stone, who themselves were on their way back home after a night out. David again lost concentration and veered into the opposite lane, Jack swerved hard to avoid him, and he did, but his car jumped the curb, he lost control, and the car skid on the grass and slammed hard into a tree, passenger side first.

David also slammed hard on the brakes as his car spun and came to a screeching halt exactly facing the Taurus. Like an old western standoff, the two cars were now idle, facing each other on an empty and quiet road.

It was dead silent as smoke was starting to come from Jack's car. David and Sarah finally awoke from the shock of what just happened.

"OH MY GOD!" David nervously shrieked, "I can't believe I just did that…Call the cops, I'm gonna go help them."

"ARE YOU CRAZY?! WE ARE DRUNK! IF THE POLICE FIND OUT, WE ARE FINISHED!" Sarah yelled back. "Just drive away quickly before anybody sees us."

David was torn, he didn't know whether to listen to Sarah or risk his life and stay to help them. The smoke had turned into a small fire under the hood of Jack's car. Lindsey was not moving, already dead since she took the brunt of the impact. But Jack was still barely breathing. He cracked his head on the window after his body recoiled when the car slammed into the tree, and his head was busted open. But he still managed to open his eyes and look at David.

"I CAN'T SIT HERE AND WATCH ANOTHER MAN DIE!" David yelled out as he released his seat belt, ready to go help him, but he was stopped by Sarah who extended her left arm and put it on David's chest.

"If you get out of this car, I'm gonna drive away!" Sarah shocked David with her ultimatum.

David paused for a few seconds. He never realized that Sarah could be this heartless. If he did go to help and Sarah drove away, how would he explain everything to the police? He thought about framing Sarah by telling the police that he happened to be walking by when this "woman" was driving recklessly and caused the accident. This idea showed exactly how fuzzy David's mind was that night. He is a smart man, but he just thought of a stupid idea because he quickly realized that Sarah would be driving away in his car, that's under his name. David frustratingly smacked his head on the steering wheel, as the precious seconds were ticking by, and Jack was about to lose his life, with David still not knowing what to do.

"WHAT ARE YOU WAITING FOR? DRIVE!" Sarah screamed at him.

David lifted his head to see that another car was coming and he just put his foot on the gas pedal and sped away, leaving Jack Stone to die in the car, next to his wife.

David let this whole incident eat him up, and consume him until it eventually ruined his life. Sarah however, was not affected by what happened, and she managed to go on with her life with no guilty conscience. The reason for that was because David had a good heart, while the same can't be said about Sarah.

PART THIRTEEN

THE QUEEN OVERTHROWS THE KING

13

After that fateful night, David's life goal was changed to helping the young kid who lost his parents because of him. Larry's goal changed to seeking retribution on the person who killed his parents. Sarah's goal never changed. It was the same as it was when she married Matt Phillips, and when she became close friends with David, and afterwards when she became Larry's wife; she was always seeking money, power, and glory. And she never let anything get in her way of achieving her goals. Even though she married Matt and Larry, David was the one who got closest to her in terms of knowing her as a person. And perhaps the best way to put how he really felt about her is to recall what he first said when Larry came over to kill him. (*"Did Sarah tell you?"*) His first assumption was that Sarah ratted him out, he knew she was untrustworthy. Once Larry's business looked like it was going to become big, she started to get close to Larry, unintentionally falling in love with him in the process. When she did get close to him, she found out that Larry had never gotten over the death of his parents. Since she knew who was responsible, she decided to play the matchmaker, and get David and Larry to meet. When David finally did meet Larry, she had to make sure that Larry somehow finds out that it was David who killed his parents without revealing the fact that she knew about it. Because David was the real architect of JL Enterprises, and Larry was the face of JL Enterprises, she felt that she had to get them out of the picture, so that she could then assume leadership of the empire. She contacted Larry's private investigator whom she knew about, to fake a speeding violation that would place David at the time and place of the accident.

("Well, my job here is done. Have a good day ma'am.")

The private investigator was speaking directly to Sarah when he said that his job was done. He was referring to the fact that Larry believed the fake evidence. Sarah then gave the P.I an envelope with even more money than what Larry had offered him. Sarah was smarter and more evil than Larry. Everything that helped to lead to her rise was planned and calculated. She never let her life be in the hands of chance. She was the master of her destiny, the star of the show. She saw everybody else as just an 'extra'. Accidently letting slip that they all used to work together was on purpose, and it was to make Larry turn on his board members. Just like Larry, she felt threatened by Jason. She thought he would rival her to take over the company once she got rid of both David and Larry. Despite Jason's goofy and laidback character, everybody knew how smart he really was. He was always the wildest partier. But when it was crunch time and they were meeting to discuss business, he would turn into the smartest person in the room. That's what scared both Larry and Sarah; if he ever stopped his party lifestyle and focused more on work, he could be dangerous. So she had to get rid of him first. She knew about Larry's bodyguard as well, and she knew that if she pushed Larry far enough, he wouldn't be afraid to take drastic action and have Jason killed.

("Did you speak to him yet? I have never seen him act the way he did, it was strange. What's going on?" Jason asked Sarah on the phone.)

("Don't worry Jason, it's nothing." Sarah replied.)

What she told Larry after that phone call with Jason was a lie. Their previous boss was never threatened by Jason. She just said that to feed the idea that Larry already had about Jason being a threat. Like a master chess player, Sarah moved the pawn into the perfect position for the king to make his move, and immediately after that conversation, the king ordered his knight to dispose of the vulnerable pawn.

But had Sarah already dug her own grave? She was messing with Larry Stone, a man who spent most of his adult life seeking revenge for the killing of his parents. And we now know how things ended up for David. What would Sarah's fate be should Larry seek retribution for the way she manipulated him? Sarah had no concerns whatsoever about what she had done, and only time will tell if messing with Larry might have been the biggest mistake of her life.

Back in the courtroom, Sarah noticed that Larry was staring at her, having just figured out in his head that Sarah was with David the night of the crash. Sarah stared back at Larry and mouthed the words, *"I'm sorry"*, although that may not have been as heartfelt as it seemed because it was followed by a smirk that was more evil than when Larry smirked at Jason before having him killed.

"Will the defendant please rise."

Larry stood up to hear his sentence, and thanks to his lawyer, and the reasoning behind Larry's actions, the judge lowered his charges from first-degree murder to voluntary manslaughter and sentenced him to 15 years in prison. Larry was escorted out of the courtroom while again staring at Sarah, and he couldn't help but laugh, laugh at the fact that he was outsmarted by Sarah.

JL Enterprises has been shaken by this scandal. Sarah, having now gotten full power with Larry in prison, decided it would be best to change the name of the company in order to get rid of the stigma that has now surrounded it. She also reverted to being called Sarah Phillips again, dropping the Stone name to distance herself from Larry. She fired all the members of the board whom she had known and worked with all those years, and promoted new people whom she had groomed within the company. The new board members were waiting in the meeting room; Sarah walked in and stood at the head of the table with her arms crossed.

"I'm sure everybody is shocked by what happened. I lost my good friend David Lawrence and our boss…my husband, is now in prison. But, there is no time to mourn or be sad about these events. We have to keep moving forward with this company, to make sure that all the hard work that Larry and David put into making this company what it is, does not go in vain. I handpicked you to form the new board of this company because I believe that you can make this transition for the company a successful one. Please, don't make me regret this decision. Is that understood?" Sarah addressed her new board members.

"Yes boss", they all replied.

"Good. Then let's get to work on making SP Enterprises even bigger and better than JL Enterprises", Sarah finally achieved her dream, Sarah Phillips had her empire.

A couple of weeks after the end of the trial, Larry had now settled into prison life. Despite the fact that he went from living in a mansion to living in cramped jail cell with another criminal, Larry was not affected by it because he was preparing his whole life for this outcome. He knew that seeking revenge would lead him to this, and he still went through with it, and he has no regrets about that. Since he had been in prison, he never got any visitors. But that was about to change. Larry was told he had a visitor, and he had no idea who it was, he didn't think it was anyone from work, and he thought it was definitely not Sarah. He went into the visiting area but he didn't see anybody that he recognized. The guard led him to his designated area where he saw a woman sitting behind the glass waiting for him. He had never seen this woman before. He was confused. He sat down and picked up the speaker.

"You don't know me. I'm Jennifer Lawrence…David's ex-wife", Jennifer introduced herself.

Larry was shocked that he was being visited by the ex-wife of the man that he killed. He didn't know what to say to her.

"It's OK, you don't have to say anything. I just came to say that I don't blame you for what happened. I blame her!" she said.

"Sarah?" Larry asked.

"I told David after the first time I met her that I got a bad vibe from her. I was there during your trial. It was the first time that I knew what David had done. I remember exactly what party he was referring to on the night of the accident. He totally changed after that night, and now I know why, and I just want to apologize for the death of your parents." Jennifer said.

"Why are you apologizing?" Larry asked her.

"Because I was supposed to go with David that night, and I didn't because I hated being around her. If I had gone then I'm sure David wouldn't have partied the way that he did, and the accident wouldn't have happened", Jennifer explained.

"It's not your fault. I was supposed to be with my parents also that night but I didn't go. If I had gone with them, things might have been different too. I guess we are both using the same logic to blame ourselves. With all the 'what if's' associated with that night, we should just accept that everything that happened that night was meant to happen. It's not my fault, and it's certainly not your fault", Larry said.

Jennifer felt that apologizing was something that she had to do. She was present at the trial and she sympathized with Larry when she found out that David had killed his parents while they were together, and she felt guilty, even though she couldn't have prevented what happened that night. Larry eased her conscience with what he said, and with that, Jennifer left thinking that this would be her one and only encounter with Larry Stone. And Larry felt the same as well, but they would meet again. Their now mutual hatred for Sarah was going to unite them into bringing her down.

PART FOURTEEN

TRUST IS A FUNNY WORD

14

Jason Kay, Larry Stone, David Lawrence - three men who together, managed to build a 500 million dollar empire. But they were no match for the evil genius that was Sarah Phillips. Jason and David ended up dead, and Larry was now in jail. She managed to pull the curtains over everyone's eyes, making everyone believe that she was an angel. Even after her master plan was achieved, she was still playing with everyone's mind.

"Boss, you came in late today for work. That's unusual, is everything ok?" An employee asked her.

"Yeah, I just stopped at the cemetery, it's been a year since David died, I thought I would visit his grave and leave some flowers", Sarah replied

"Oh, I'm sorry. I thought maybe she kept you up all night", the employee replied.

She did actually visit David's grave, but it was only so that she could tell people about it and make them believe that she had a good heart. It has been a year now since Larry killed David, and it was the first time she had visited David's grave. But there is one thing that she had wanted to do for a while now, and that was to visit Larry in prison. Not because she misses him or wants to check on him, but it was because she felt that there was something that he needed to know. It would be the first time that the two would see each other since Larry's trial. She entered the visitor's area and saw Larry already there, sitting behind the glass panel. His beard has gotten thicker and he had his head shaved bald. Larry has been staring at her since she walked in with no emotion on his face. She sat down and grabbed the speaker to talk to Larry. Larry has still not picked up his speaker; he was just staring at her. He made her wait a while before he finally picked it up.

"...Hi...how are you?" Sarah hadn't seen her husband in a year, she lied to him, manipulated him into killing David, which resulted in him going to prison, and that was the first thing she said to him.

"Sarah, I never quite got you. You always seemed so sweet and innocent, but you betrayed your oldest friends and let your husband, sorry, ex-husband end up in jail. And now after a year, you come here and ask me how I am?! You don't care how I'm doing! The only reason you came here is because you got something to say to me right? So go ahead and say it!" Larry told her.

"Larry, let's be honest, you're not really that smart. Did you really believe that you were the one in charge that whole time? You should have guessed that someone else was leading us. It's not my fault that you were easy to manipulate. But, I didn't do anything wrong, Larry. You always wanted to kill the man responsible for your parent's death. I just led you to him!" Sarah replied. "But you are right about one thing, I do have something I want to say to you. Actually, it's something I want to show you." Sarah said.

Sarah reached into her purse and pulled out a photo and pushed it up on the glass. It was a photo of a baby girl, Larry's daughter.

"I never told you this, but I found out I was pregnant a couple of days before you killed David. I was planning to surprise you with the news but I never had the chance. I named her Allie Violet Stone. I named her after your sister, that's what you told me your parents were gonna name her", Sarah told Larry.

Larry was left speechless. He raised his hand against the glass looking at his daughter's eyes.

"I'm sorry," Sarah said as Larry still hasn't blinked, keeping an intense star into his daughters eyes.

"Larry..." Sarah wanted to get a reaction from Larry, who has spent a minute now without saying anything.

"Why didn't you tell me?" Larry finally said something.

Larry was angered, he was biting his lips, and his leg was shaking. For the first time since killing David, he was regretting what he did. When he killed David, he felt that he had nothing to lose. He never really cared for his wealth or even Sarah. If he had known that Sarah was pregnant, he would've had something to live for. He might have forgotten seeking retribution and instead focused on his child. It turned out to be a stroke of luck for Sarah that she never had the chance to tell him she was pregnant. If she had told him in time, none of this would have happened.

"HOW COULD YOU DO THIS TO ME?!"
Larry was still angry, as his voice got louder. There was
no doubt in his mind that she was actually showing him
a picture of his daughter. There was no reason that Sarah
would try to manipulate Larry anymore, so he believed
that she was telling the truth, and she was.

Larry got out of his chair, he punched the glass partition
and was still shouting at Sarah, who had no response. It
was the first time that Sarah actually felt bad. The
guards came over and dragged Larry by his arms to take
him back to his cell. But Larry wasn't going away
easily, or quietly.

"YOU TAKE CARE OF HER!! YOU TAKE
CARE OF MY DAUGHTER OR I SWEAR TO GOD I
WILL KILL YOU!!! IF YOU EVER HURT MY
DAUGHTER I WILL HAVE YOU BURIED NEXT TO
DAVID! YOU HEAR ME, YOU WATCH YOUR
BACK…" Larry yelled out.

The visiting area became quiet as Larry disappeared
through the doors leading back to the cell area. The rest
of the visitors and prisoners looked over at Sarah.

"Ma'am, are you okay?" A guard came over to
comfort her. "Don't worry about what he said, he can't
harm you."

But Sarah wasn't afraid, she felt bad about what she had
done to Larry. She took away his chance to be a father.
This caring moment however, was just that; a moment,

it didn't last long, it didn't convince Sarah that she needs to change her ways.

"…I'm fine." Sarah calmly said, as she put the photo back in her purse and left the prison.

It was not easy to break Sarah, and this incident did nothing to affect her focus and dedication towards her company. The improvements that Sarah had made at SP Enterprises astonished the financial experts who predicted the worse for the company after the scandal that befell them. With all the extra baggage out of the way; Jason, Larry, and David, she was able to put her full concentration into the business, which was bad for Allie, who spent most of her time with her nanny.

"First off, I would like to thank you for taking the time to give us this exclusive interview", cameras were set up in Sarah's office, as Forbes magazine had come over to interview her.

"It's my pleasure", responded Sarah.

"SP Enterprises has made major strides since you took over. You have now moved into the top 10 companies listed by Forbes, and for you personally, gracing the cover of Forbes magazine with the title 'The most powerful woman in America'. How did you manage to achieve this after what you have been through?" The interviewer asked.

"Well, everybody that knows me knows that I'm a very determined person. When the company went through what happened we were all shocked and saddened. But having a business mind like myself, my first thought was damage control. We have a multimillion-dollar company behind us so we had to quickly shift our focus to the well-being of the company. The first thing that I thought was important was to let our shareholders know that our previous owner was not the main cause for our success and that we can manage without him. We contacted them and showed them our current projects that we were working on, and that we will still finish with me in charge", Sarah answered.

"When you did take charge, you made two drastic decisions. One was firing all your board members, and second was changing the name of the company. What was the thought process behind those two decisions?" The interviewer asked.

"A new start! We had to move on swiftly and show everybody that this company wasn't all about our previous owner and to show that, I had to get rid of his board members and make my own team. And the name, well, I didn't want people to hear the name we previously had and say 'oh that's the company that had this, this, and this happen to it' so I decided to change the name just to show people it's my company now", Sarah said.

"You certainly seem determined! What's next for you and your company?"

"The thing that I always wanted to do is go international. We have proved that we can dominate here in America. The next logical step is going abroad. We have a few projects lined up that would help us achieve that goal", Sarah said.

"So when we interview next time, we would have to change your title to the most powerful women in the world?" The interviewer smiled.

"No, I think I need to run for president in order to receive that title", Sarah said laughing.

Larry thought that Sarah's last visit would be the last time anybody would come to visit him. But he would get a string of surprise visitors. The last visit would be from his former lawyer, who was about to discover something odd with all the paperwork that belonged to Larry. But the first visitor was Steve Nichols. He never visited Larry in prison because he was going through health problems, but he was finally feeling fit enough to go see him.

"Uncle Steve, I didn't expect to see you", Larry greeted him.

"How are you doing son?" Steve asked.

"I'm in prison, so I could be better. What about you? What happened to you?" Asked Larry.

"Don't worry about me, it's just old age!" Steve replied.

"How's Aunt Judy?" Larry asked.

"She's disappointed in you. She didn't expect you to turn out to be a killer", Steve told him.

"Is that why she's not here with you?" Larry asked.

"Whenever I talk about you she changes the subject. I couldn't go forever without coming to see you, and I tried to convince her to come, but...I don't think that will ever happen", Steve replied.

"...Are you disappointed in me?" Larry asked.

"If I was you, I would have emptied my gun into that bastard! But it's good to see that all the shooting practice paid off, you killed him with one shot", Steve said.

"Send my regards to Aunt Judy, will you? Tell her I'm sorry, I just did what I had to do", Larry said.

"I will". Steve replied.

As time passed and Allie was growing up, she began to talk. This made Sarah have another awful moment because her father was missing out on seeing his daughter grow up, and Allie had yet to see her father. She felt that she should at least see him, so she set up a visit to go see Larry in prison. She wasn't really looking forward to the encounter. The only thing that she was looking forward to was knowing that Larry would become an emotional wreck when he sees his daughter for the first time. Sarah arrived at the prison and waited for Larry. Larry walked out with a grin on his face, but that quickly changed to shock. He knew he was going to see Sarah, but he wasn't expecting to see his daughter sitting on her lap. Sarah got up and introduced Larry to his daughter, and with no glass barriers this time so that Larry could be able to hold his daughter.

"This is Allie Violet Stone. Say hi to your daddy Allie", Sarah said.

"…My daughter", Larry reached his arm out to hold Allie. But his hands were handcuffed and chained to his ankles.

"…Please, I want to hold my daughter", Larry said to the guard with his arms raised.

The guard looked at Sarah not knowing whether to release his handcuffs or not.

"It's okay," Sarah told the guard.

The guard proceeded to unlock Larry's handcuffs and Larry held his daughter for the first time.

"Hi…" Larry said with a tear rolling down his cheek and a smile on his face. He hadn't stopped smiling since he had seen Allie. All the stress that he had been feeling faded away as he was holding his baby girl. But regret was a feeling that has taken over him now. Regret that he could never be a father to his daughter. And regret that he would never see his parents holding their granddaughter. He only held her for a minute before giving her back to Sarah.

"I'm sorry…" Sarah said.

But Larry didn't care to hear what Sarah had to say. He didn't even look at her when he gave back Allie. He just turned around and asked the guard to take him back to his cell. The woman who mesmerized him with her looks the first time that he saw her was now a woman whom he couldn't stand to look at anymore.

The train of visitors coming to see Larry was finally dropping off its last passenger. Paul Beigler, Larry's former lawyer, hasn't spoken to Larry since the trial, so Larry was surprised when he received a call asking to meet him. Paul told him that it was urgent that they meet, because he was about to share with him the odd thing that he found among Larry's papers. The visitor's area had now become a frequent home for Larry, and he again entered to see a visitor waiting for him to take his seat behind the glass partition this time.

"What is it?" Larry asked.

"I don't know if you heard but I'm retiring. I'm clearing my office of all the paperwork that I had", Paul told Larry.

"Oh, I didn't hear about that. But you had a great run, you were my dad's lawyer and then you became mine. Thanks for being with me for such a long time Paul", Larry said.

"It was my pleasure, Larry", Paul replied.

"Did you just come here to tell me that, because I see papers in your hand, are those for me?" asked Larry.

"Yeah, they are. As I was throwing away the files I had, I came across yours. For some reason, I decided to look it over and I found a document that was interesting…I really don't know how this slipped past you, because I don't think you looked at it carefully", Paul said.

"…What document?" A confused Larry asked.

"The company was originally in your dad's name, but after he passed away, did you do the proper paperwork to change it under your ownership?" Paul asked him.

"…I…yeah I think we did. Those guys came up with the new business plan, I oversaw it and gave them the approval to go ahead with it. Why?" Larry was genuinely puzzled now.

"Who completed the procedure?" Paul asked.

"It was on Jason's computer so I guess it was him," Larry answered.

"I thought you would say that. I found a copy of the original paper with the business plan and owner for the company, check out the signature next to the title of 'owner'," Paul said.

The lawyer lifted the paper and pressed it on the glass. Larry looked over it and he remembered it was the same document that Jason had showed him. He looked at the signature and it was just the initials JK.

"What?!" Larry was shocked to see Jason's initials.

"I'm afraid you were played from day one Larry. Jason Kay made himself the owner of the company!" Paul said.

"How?!" Larry was still shocked.

"I don't know, he must have signed it himself after you guys left or something," Paul said. He too, was dumbfounded by this new revelation.

"So Jason took my dad's company and put his name on it?" Larry asked.

"Yup, and he did it legally since you signed this paper." Paul lifted another paper and pressed it on the glass. What Larry had signed was an agreement that he relinquishes his dads company to Jason. "You should never sign anything without letting your lawyer look at it." Paul said.

"…What does that mean? Jason is dead, if he was the owner and not me, then who is the owner now?" Larry asked the 500-million dollar question.

PART FIFTEEN

CALL ME SIR OR MASTER

15

After David, Frank, and Jason met that day to discuss David starting his own business, it was settled that David was finally going to fulfil their wishes. But due to the accident, things had to change, and David only trusted one person enough to inform them of the change of plans. David, with a scruffy five o'clock shadow, a shirt that was not tucked in, and bags under his eyes, was anxiously sitting in a cafe, tapping his legs while waiting to meet with the person he trusted the most.

"Thanks for meeting me today Jason," David told Jason Kay as he arrived late and took his seat.

"No problem buddy. We haven't seen you at work lately, is everything OK?" Jason asked.

"I am just working on something. Do you want to be the master?" David asked him.

"You're serious? Don't joke about this man!" Jason said.

"It's no joke, let's get things going. But, there is a slight change in the plans. There is this kid called Larry Stone, I was friends with his dad, and both his parents passed away recently", David lied that he was a friend of Larry's father.

"Oh man, sorry to hear that. But what does he have to do with you starting your own business?" Jason asked.

"I have been following him and he is now in charge of his dad's business. I studied his business and what his dad started was pretty good, I feel like the blueprint for it can be used to build my own business", David said.

"Go on…" Jason said.

"Look, you guys will go work for him and build what his dad had already started and I will help out. He probably doesn't have enough money to pay you guys a good salary, but I'm willing to pay you guys. He needs help, and it will be a win-win situation for everyone; he can get the help he needs and you guys will finally work for a company that I'm in charge of", David explained.

"Why am I feeling that there is something missing? I feel like there is a big 'but' coming. You know I don't like big buts with a single T!" Jason said.

"But, I'm not going to be directly involved. I will be in charge but he mustn't know that. I had a fall-out with his dad a few years ago and I don't think he will want to work with me", David lied about the reason he didn't want Larry to know that he was involved.

"So let me get this straight; he will just be the figurehead, and on paper I will be the owner like we agreed, and you will be the architect but only he will not know that, am I right?" Jason asked.

"Yes, that's the plan. Just don't tell anyone that the company is going to be in your name, especially Sarah", David said.

"I am not surprised that you singled her out, you feel that she's not trustworthy too?" Jason asked.

"She is too ambitious and as much as I hate to say it, a little heartless too. That's a bad combination, she would do anything to get what she wants. I know she wants to be in charge, and it will be bad for everyone if she is. So don't tell her", David explained.

"But I can still tell Frank, right? He was with us when we first agreed that I will be in charge of your company", Jason asked.

"No, the plan has changed now, everyone needs to believe that Larry, on paper, is the man in charge. They will, of course, know that I'm the architect, but no one should know your true role Jason, not even Frank! Larry is too young to deal with being the owner, so it's your responsibility to take care of things like you said you would until he is ready", David said.

"Oh man, you mean I am gonna be the master and I can't tell anyone about it? No one will know? That's torture!" Jason complained.

"Find someone else to tell, just don't tell them. Your word Jason", David said as he extended his hand.

"My word", Jason said as both men shook hands, and came up with the plan to build Larry's empire. David saw these changes as mandatory in order for everything to work smoothly, and it did work. But what he also told Jason that day was that when Larry is old enough and ready to be in charge, he will give up his title as owner to Larry. But, this was a promise that

Jason failed to keep and he remained the owner until his death. The idea that he was in charge went to his head and he couldn't let go of it. David's alterations to their master plan were a stroke of genius. His reservations about Sarah were spot on, he knew her better than anyone else, and he knew it was in everyone's best interest that she doesn't know what's going on, and more importantly, that she never takes charge.

Back to the present day, Larry is still looking at that paper that showed Jason as the owner, confused, trying to figure out who legally became the owner after Jason died.

"Okay, but this is just the copy, where was the original document?" Larry asked.

"I don't know…" replied his lawyer.

"You think Sarah has it?" Asked Larry.

"No I don't think so. I feel like we are just on the surface here, there is some far weirder shit going on." Paul said.

"What do you mean?" Larry inquired.

"Well, two very important pieces of papers are missing; the original document of ownership and Jason's will." He explained.

"Jason's will is missing?" Larry asked.

"Yeah, it went missing after he died. You didn't know about that?"

"No, I couldn't care less about him or his will."

"Well, think about it now that you know he was the owner. Don't you think it's strange that the will of the owner of a multi-million dollar company just happened to vanish after his death? What was written in his will about him being the owner and who should succeed him?"

"You're right, sounds fishy." Larry concurred.

"I spoke with Jason's lawyer and he confirmed that there was a will but it went missing after his death. So there must be something in that will connected with him being the owner. Huh, if only you had a private investigator to solve this mystery", Paul joked.

"…The PI! Whatever happened to him?" Asked Larry.

"I heard that he retired a long time ago. After that nice payday that he got from you, he didn't need to work anymore", he answered.

"And? Where is he now?" Larry asked again.

"Nobody knows. He could be in Barbados getting tanned for all we know. But why the sudden concern about the PI? Who was he really? You think he might be involved with the disappearance of the documents?" Paul asked.

"I made a mistake with him, I gave him too much freedom to poke around the company, he had access to everything. I know he was friends with Jason and his lawyer, that's how I met him. He came a few times to Jason's parties. I should have known he was gonna turn out to be a snake. Now that I think about it more, he was the only one close with both Jason and his lawyer. If the documents were stolen, I wouldn't be surprised if he knows something about it. We have to find him", said Larry.

"How do you expect to find him?" Asked his lawyer.

"…We need a snake to catch a snake. I know a guy who could help", Larry grinned.

PART SIXTEEN

THE TWO ANOMALIES

16

Sarah was the kind of person who snooped around to see what Larry was hiding. She knew about the private investigator that he had hired to look into his parent's death, and she also knew about the bodyguard. Because she was involved in the death of his parents, she feared the PI might find that she was with David that night. She decided it would be in her best interests to get close to the PI in order to get him on her side.

"Mrs. Stone… I didn't think I'd run into you here", Martin, the PI, said as he was sitting having coffee.

Larry had given him a meaningless position in his company just so people won't get suspicious about him always being there and they won't figure out his real job. But Sarah knew, and she didn't run into him by accident. She pulled a chair and sat with him.

"I see you spend a lot of time in the company, you're a real hard worker," Sarah said.

"…Um... thanks", Martin replied.

"It's surprising too since you already have another job," Sarah said to him.

"I'm sorry… what do you mean?" Martin said.

"It's okay Martin, Larry told me about you. I know you are a private investigator", Sarah said.

"How do you know, he said nobody knows?!" Martin asked.

"I'm not just anybody Martin, I'm his wife; of course he would tell me", Sarah told him.

Having now blown his cover, the two of them chatted for a while about work until Sarah dropped the whole formal, work atmosphere of this encounter by talking about his personal life.

"You're not married, right? I'm sorry I'm just asking because I don't see a ring on your finger", Sarah asked him.

"No ma'am, I'm divorced", Martin answered.

"Oh, I'm sorry to hear that. She must be stupid because you seem like a really great guy. You can drop the whole ma'am, Mrs. Stone thing, we are not at work. You can call me Sarah", Sarah was trying to flirt with the PI who was much older than her, in his late forties.

"Thank you, Sarah", Martin smiled.

Sarah managed to get real close with Martin, and being a beautiful woman with a strong mind, he couldn't help but fall for her seductions. Weeks pass and the meetings increased, in public and in private as well. This was not something that bothered Sarah because she got what she wanted. The PI was now in the palm of her hand; a new puppet for her to control. She just waited until the time was right before executing her plan that would lead to the literal execution of David. Sarah never really bothered to get Larry's bodyguard on her side as well. And she would live to regret that decision. Not that she could have gotten him on her side because there was a personal connection between Larry and his bodyguard.

Larry first met his bodyguard when he was 17 years old. After his parents died, Steve, his dad's shooting partner offered Larry a job in his security company. He even decided to invite him for a day at the office to see the place.

"This is where we work, it's not a lovely place to work, but I got the best guys here and they make this place feel like home. This is our best employee; it might be biased coming from me since I'm his dad. Larry, this is my son, Mark, although everyone calls him Snake. Son this is Larry Stone, I told you about him", Steve said.

"Yeah, Larry, how are you?" Asked Mark as he shook hands with Larry.

"I'm okay. Snake, like Solid Snake?" Larry laughed, referring to the iconic video game character, who is a special ops soldier that would go on life threatening missions on his own.

"That's actually why they call me that, they all say I'm just like him", answered Mark.

"Wow seriously! You're a one man army too, special force in the CIA or something?" Larry questioned.

"If I told you, I'd have to kill you!" Mark jokingly responded.

Larry laughed, the first time that he has laughed since his parents died. He liked Mark's personality even though he did feel intimidated by him, as he is a scary guy. With all the other employees wearing formal or semi-formal attire at work, Mark was casually dressed as he always is. He was wearing a white tank top that highlighted his ripped arms, and worn out blue jeans. His arms and face had a few scars, and his face did not convey that this was a man in his mid 30's, with wear and tear on his face that would make you guess that this was at least a 50 year old man. His look was stone cold with striking blue eyes, and he barely smiled even when he would tell a joke. Even though Larry refused to work with Steve in his security company, Steve and Mark would remain close as they helped look after him. Mark was a former Marine, who lived by the motto "Semper Fi", which meant always loyal, and was the motto for the Marines. He would never turn his back on family, and that's what he viewed Larry; as his little brother. When Mark wanted to meet Larry in the park all those years ago after Larry had gotten into a fight, he wanted to ask him a few questions. He had only met Larry twice before, but on those two occasions, he felt something in Larry that he wanted to make sure was true.

With a man walking his dog and two women jogging, Mark was sitting on a bench in the Park waiting for Larry to come. He arrived, with a bandaged nose and black eye, and he slowly approached the bench from behind. Mark sensed him and he looked over his shoulder.

"You're here early," Mark told Larry.

"Yeah you scared me on the phone, I didn't want to be late," Larry replied.

"Don't be scared, I'm not gonna hurt you," Mark said as Larry sat on the bench next to him.

"Those were pretty big men you were fighting with. Why were you fighting with them?" Mark asked.

"I accidentally bumped into them...I didn't want to fight them but...they made fun of my mother", Larry explained.

"And the mention of your mother made you decide to get into a fight you should've known you were gonna lose?" Mark asked.

"I wasn't thinking straight, I didn't think about winning or losing that fight. I guess I just lost control of my emotions and did what I had to do", Larry said.

"You're still upset about your parent's death?" Mark asked.

"Of course I am! I don't think I will ever stop being upset about what happened to them", Larry said.

With each question, Mark felt that he was getting closer to hearing what he wanted to hear.

"...I'm not going to stop looking for whoever did this. I don't care how long it takes. When I do find out who killed my parents...I'm gonna kill them", Larry said.

And with that answer, Mark heard what he wanted to hear. Mark had a feeling that it was something involving his parents that made Larry get into that fight. And he thought that if Larry was crazy enough to get into a fight with two much stronger men because they made fun of his mother, then he might do something even crazier and go after the person who killed his parents. Seeing that Mark has stopped asking questions now, and he was just staring off into the distance, Larry wanted to go back home. As Larry said goodbye, he put his arms on the bench to lift himself off it, but Mark grabbed Larry by his forearm and held him in a firm grip. Larry looked back with a frightened look. Mark had the same stone cold look on his face. He wasn't looking at Larry, he was just looking straight.

"Listen, Larry, you're a good kid, don't do anything stupid," Mark said while still gripping Larry's arm, "You keep looking for who killed your parents, and when you find them, you just tell me...I will take care of it."

Mark promised as he finally looked at Larry. Larry, now looking at Mark's piercing blue eyes, realized that Mark's mysterious and cold character wasn't just for show. He wasn't just a bodyguard, he really was a snake; he was a hit man.

PART SEVENTEEN

MONEY V.S LOYALTY

17

Larry formed a close bond with Mark and he used his intimidating presence to protect not only himself but his empire as well. Larry met the PI through Jason, and he discreetly talked to him at one of Jason's parties to hire him to look into his parent's death.

During the time that the PI was secretly working at JL Enterprises, he never once bumped into Mark, who himself spent a considerable time at the company while serving as Larry's bodyguard. But the stage was now set for the two most ambiguous and shady characters in this whole story to take centre stage. But how did they come to this role? How did we reach the point where Mark and Martin would hold the fate of everyone in this story in their hands? Mark was driven to this point by loyalty. But nobody quite knows why Martin played the pivotal role that he did.

Larry now suspected that the PI had something to do with the missing will and original document that showed Jason as the owner. So he called Mark, or Snake as he liked to call him, and told him to get information about the PI. After a couple of weeks, Mark came to visit Larry in prison along with Larry's lawyer.

"So, what did you find out?" Larry asked.

"Well, first of all, the name on his calling card is fake; his name is not Martin. I checked if he had made any phone calls from his office while he was working for you, and he had just made one phone call; it was to Jason's lawyer", replied Snake.

"You're kidding me! He's got the documents right?" Larry asked.

"I paid Jason's lawyer a little visit and he was adamant that the documents were stolen from his office.

When I asked if it was possible that 'Martin' may have stolen them, he said it's possible. He told me he called him to ask about Jason's will, that Mr. Stone asked him to look for it", Snake replied.

"What? I never told him to do that?!" Larry said.

"Wait, how did you manage to get all this from him? I talked to him before, and he barely said anything to me." Paul asked.

"I know how to get people to talk!" Snake replied.

"So what are we gonna do now?" Larry asked.

"I will find him", Snake replied.

"How in God's name are you gonna do that!? You don't even know his real name!"Paul said.

"I said I will find him!" Snake confidently said.

"But how can we be certain that even if he did take them, he hasn't shredded them already?" Larry asked.

"No, if in fact, he did take them, then he wouldn't be stupid to shred them. With those documents, he has Sarah in the palm of his hands. We know that he loves money, and with those documents, he can blackmail her anytime he wants", Paul replied.

"It's all up to you then Snake, go find him...but I'm in jail now, I can't pay you for what you are about to do", Larry told Snake.

"I never did this for the money Larry. You know that", Snake replied.

"...Yeah, I know...sorry", an embarrassed Larry replied.

"...Semper Fi..." Snake said as he got up from his chair ready to begin his next mission.

Snake set off to find the private investigator; it was his turn to be detective. He thought the first place to start was at SP Enterprises. There is a big chance that Sarah knew the PI's real name, but there was no way Snake was gonna go knock on her door and ask her. But since the PI spent a lot of time at the company, maybe he got close to other people as well. Snake knew some people also from his time there so he contacted them. It was a group of three guys and he met them after they finished work. He was waiting for them outside the building, as the three suited men came out of the revolving doors and went to greet him.

"You guys remember Martin?" He asked them.

"Yeah, he quit or something, right?" One of them said.

"Actually, he retired. The guy stole some money from the company and I'm...We're trying to find him",

Snake lied to them about the reason he was looking for him.

"Seriously?!" They asked in shock.

"Did any of you guys get close to him, got to know where he lived or something?" He asked them again.

"We know that he was close with Sarah, we would see them a lot after work hanging out", one of them said.

"They did more than just hanging out if you know what I mean", another guy jumped in.

"Sarah and Martin?" Snake asked.

"Yup, I saw them with my own eyes going into an apartment together, but these guys wouldn't believe me", replied the guy.

"And where is that apartment?" Snaked asked. He was expecting that it would be an apartment that was far away and he would have to go search for it. But to his surprise, the guy just lifted his right arm and with his index finger pointed to a building just down the street.

"...It's the one right there." The guy said. Snake got a lucky break, he had gotten something to work with now.

He went to the apartment building and spoke with the landlord asking for information about his previous tenants. With Snake's known persuasive approach, the landlord showed him the names of the previous tenants who stayed there. The landlord was certain that nobody named Martin stayed in his building. That meant he probably used his real name. He was hoping he could circle a few names that could have been him based on the time frame when the PI was working at the company. But he didn't need to circle any names, as he got another lucky break, and he managed to figure out which name it was the second he saw it.

"Brennan! Alan Brennan!"A shocked Snake whispered to himself.

Brennan was a name only Snake would have caught because that was the last name of Jason Kay's lawyer whom he had interviewed. He decided to pay Eric Brennan another visit, but this time, he went straight to his home. He unlocked the front door and went looking for him. The house looked empty, until he heard someone speaking in a room to his right. He opened the door and he would find Eric in his office talking on the phone. With a startled look on his face, he quickly ended the call.

"…I'll call you back", the lawyer said as Snake closed the door and locked it.

"You didn't expect to see me again did you? It seems you weren't honest with me; that was a mistake. Because when people lie to me I get angry, and you don't want that to happen", Snake warned him.

"…I…I don't know what you are talking about?" Eric responded in fear.

"Alan Brennan. Is he related to you by any chance?" Snake asked.

The lawyer was quiet, stunned how he managed to get that name. Snake pulled out a gun that was tucked in the back of his pants and pointed it at the lawyer.

"Hmm, first you lie and now you don't say anything. You really know how to piss me off", Snake told him, still pointing the gun at Eric.

"OK, OK, he's my older brother, please don't kill me!" The lawyer pleaded.

"See that wasn't so hard. Now, where is your older brother?" Snake asked him.

"I have no idea…" he replied.

"Hmmm" Snake didn't say anything.

"I swear I'm telling the truth, I...I haven't spoken to him in a year, I'll show you my phone record if you want!" The lawyer said.

"Did he take the missing papers?" Snake asked.

"…Yes…yes he did. He said that these papers could be dangerous if I keep them with me. He said people might come looking for them eventually, and I didn't want to be a part of this. I know that Sarah and Larry are dangerous people…I…I didn't want to be involved I swear. So he decided it was best that these documents disappeared with him." The lawyer confessed.

"Disappear where?" Asked Snake.

"…Miami…" the lawyer answered.

"What was written in Jason's will?" Snake asked again.

"…Larry Stone relinquished control of his company to Jason. It was him that was the owner all along", the lawyer said.

"Yeah, I know that already", Snake replied.

"…Well, he named his successor in his will, and it wasn't Larry or Sarah. Huh, people are calling her the most powerful woman in America, but she doesn't know that she is not the legal owner of that company…A will takes precedence…the company went into the hands of another family", the lawyer said.

"Who?" Snake asked.

The lawyer told him the name and once he had gotten all the information that he wanted from him, Snake saw that the lawyer wasn't useful anymore, and to make sure that there were no loose ends, he thought it would be best to dispose of him now. So without saying a word, he fired two shots right in the middle of Eric's chest.

Now that he knew the PI's real name and location, the rest was easy for a man like Snake. It wasn't long after arriving in Miami that he found out where he lived. He went to his place, a villa along Miami Beach, but he noticed a lot of cars in the driveway and loud music coming from inside the villa. Apparently, Alan was having a party; he was literally enjoying his retirement by having parties every now and then. But Snake did what he does best; he didn't want to barge in with all the people inside, he didn't want there to be any witnesses. So he waited outside the house, hiding behind some bushes so that no one could see him. Just like a true snake waiting for the perfect opportunity to strike its prey. The party lasted till early morning, as he saw the guests leave one by one, most of whom were drunk, and most of them were women. When the last car left the driveway, he knew that this was his moment to strike.

Nobody bothered to lock the front door after they left, and he just turned the knob and was easily inside the house. The lights were off on the ground floor, and the only light was coming from the TV that was still on with the volume very low. Clothes were strewn on the floor, chips and cigar ash were covering the tables, and empty beer cans were all over the floor.

He slowly moved further, with his gun already in his hand, he saw a guy passed out on the couch in front of the TV. He let him be as he seemed too passed out to cause any problem. He slowly went up the winding staircase, and when he reached the top, he heard the flushing of the toilet, from the bathroom to his left. With his gun ready, he waited against the rails to see who would come out of the toilet. The door opened and Alan Brennan stumbled out.

"What are you still doing here? The party's over go home", Alan drunkenly told him, not recognizing who he was.

There was one spotlight lit in the ceiling, but Snake was standing behind the area it was lighting, which made his face in the shadows. Snake did not say anything, and he just stood there in the darkness.

"Huh…too drunk to drive? Okay you can crash here for the night, but this is the last I'm gonna let you guys sleep over for free, you are gonna have to pay next time", Alan told him.

Snake wanted to end this little charade, so he took one step forward so that he was right under the spotlight. When the spotlight illuminated his face, Alan began to recall who he was.

"…Wait…I know you…where have I seen you before?" Alan was taking a few seconds, trying to remember who he was. "In New York… you worked at JL Enterprises… you're…you're the…"

Alan finally recognized him as Larry Stone's bodyguard, and he quickly turned and ran towards his room with Snake chasing him. As they both ran into the room, Snake caught up with him and grabbed him from behind and slammed him to the floor. With Alan on his back, Snake punched his face as he sat on top of him and began yelling at him.

"WHERE IS IT?! WHERE IS JASON'S WILL?" Snake yelled.

"… I don't know what you are talking about I swear…" Alan begged.

Snake then grabbed his shirt and pulled him up off the floor and with both his hands grabbing the front of Alan's shirt he shoved him up against the closet.

"Don't play stupid with me, I know you took Jason's will. What were you trying to gain huh? You were gonna use that to blackmail Sarah?" Snake asked him.

"…What? Blackmail her? No… no, you got it all wrong. I didn't do this to damage Sarah. I wanted to protect her", Alan answered.

"Protect her?" Snake asked.

"…Yes…I loved Sarah…I…my brother showed me Jason's will right after he died…before anybody else could see it…I knew that if the will came out it would ruin Sarah's plan to take over, and she would lose everything. So I helped her again, but without her knowing this time", confessed Alan.

"Again?" Snake asked.

"…The speeding ticket…the one that helped Larry figure out that it was David…it was fake. She told me to do it. She gave me the location, the time, and the date," Alan confessed.

"Do you still have that will?" Snake asked.

Alan didn't say anything. Snake put his left arm against Alan's throat, and with his right hand, he raised his gun and aimed it at Alan's forehead.

"I said do you still have that will?!" Snake asked again.

"…It's…it's in a briefcase, in the closet", Alan gasped.

"Get that briefcase", Snake pulled him off away from the closet he had pressed him against, turned him around and shoved him face first towards the closet.

Alan, with his arms shaking, opened the closet and reached to the top shelf. Underneath some old jackets was a raggedy old briefcase with a single number lock on it. Alan took the briefcase and was now on his knees, looking up at Snake. With his hands shaking, Alan put the combination to open the lock. He lifted the lid open and took out the papers and handed them to Snake

"…Here…take them…just don't shoot me", with blood running from his nose, Alan surrendered the documents to Snake in hopes that he will spare his life.

Snake grabbed the papers to make sure they were the real documents. With the documents in his hands he was now ready to finish what he started.

"Shoot you? No, you got it wrong also. I'm not gonna shoot you, that would be too easy", Snake said.

Snake then punched Alan again with his empty right hand, and knocked him to the ground. He tucked his gun in the back in his pants and dragged Alan by his shirt out of the bedroom and to the edge of the winding stairs. He lifted Alan with both hands so that his back was facing the stairs. This second punch dazed Alan and he was barely standing on weak legs.

"It seemed like you had one hell of a party Alan. It's a shame though that you had too much to drink. Cause you know, accidents can happen when you are too drunk", Snake was brilliantly evoking what started this whole saga all those years ago. It was David who was drunk that caused the accident that killed Larry's parents; now Alan is the one that is drunk, and his "accident" will bring about the end of this saga. Snake then gave him the slightest of pushes, sending him tumbling down the stairs, breaking his neck along the way, and leaving his lifeless body lying at the foot of the stairs, all the while the passed out guest remained sleeping on the couch. It took him a couple of months, but Snake managed to get the papers that would bring down Sarah Phillips.

PART EIGHTEEN

THE OWNER

18

"Its Mark", Mark was in a phone booth talking to Paul Beigler.

"Hey, you are back. What happened?" Paul asked.

"I got what you guys wanted. We need to meet Larry."

"Alright, we can do it tomorrow afternoon."

"OK, and another thing, tell David's wife to come as well."

"Why? What was in the will?"

"I will tell you tomorrow." Mark said as he hung up the phone.

Snake completed his mission and made his way back to New York. He spoke with Paul and arranged to meet him with Larry. What was surprising to Paul was that Snake asked him to contact Jennifer Lawrence so that she would be present as well. Snake didn't tell him the contents of the will; he said it was best with everyone present. Paul contacted Jennifer and she agreed to come. They all met up in the prison visiting area waiting for the guards to escort Larry to them. He arrived and took his seat at the table.

"So, I assume everything went well?" asked Larry.

"Yeah, I got what you wanted. Why don't you read out what's written in Jason's will", Snake handed the will to Paul.

"OK…last will and testament, Jason Fisher Kay… (Quickly skims through the paper). Ah, here it is.

I leave my car and beach house to my brother…as for JL Enterprises, I was entrusted to be the owner of the company since Larry was too young…but if you are reading this will then it means I'm dead, and I have the power to name my successor...my successor should be David Lawrence. He was the architect behind the success of JL Enterprises, and he trusted me to be the owner, but I turned my back on him. So I am giving him what rightfully belongs to him."

They all remained quiet, trying to let what they just heard sink in. When Jason declined to help David come work with them, he felt bad. In the power trip that he was on, Jason had forgotten that David was the real reason behind the success of the company, and he was one of his closest friends. To soothe the guilt that Jason was feeling, he contacted his lawyer and along with his brother, they went to make their respective wills. He felt that naming David as the successor to the company was the least that he could do, he was just giving him and his family, the company that he built.

"…I…I didn't expect that…so…who…so David is… I'm sorry could you just explain this because I'm a little confused." Larry told Paul.

"Hmm Jason died before David right? So when that happened, according to his will, David Lawrence became the owner", explained his lawyer.

"So when I shot and killed David, I actually killed the owner of MY own company?" Larry just realized. But actually, he had killed the owner of his company twice, Jason Kay, of course, being the first.

"Yes, that's right", his lawyer said.

"…Does that mean that when David died…as his wife, the company became mine…am I the owner? Is that why you guys brought me here?" Jennifer was confused as well. Snake also believed that she is the owner now, that's why he asked for her to be there. But they were both wrong.

"Correct me if I am wrong, but you were already divorced at the time of David's death, right? So you can't inherit it…his kids would!" The lawyer explained to her.

"…What? My daughter?!" Said a shocked Jennifer.

"Yes Mrs. Lawrence, your daughter is the rightful heir to a multimillion Dollar company", Paul said to the astonishment of everyone present.

The true heir to the company turned out to be someone that nobody expected; the only offspring of David Lawrence, Bonnie.

"Mrs. Lawrence, where is your daughter?" Paul asked.

"She's in law school in Boston," Jennifer answered.

"She has to come to New York and file a lawsuit against Sarah Phillips. She is the only one that can bring her down now", Paul told her.

"Are you sure that it will work? Could she seriously win?" Jennifer asked.

"Ma'am, this paper that I have in my hand is what we call a slam dunk. There is no way that Sarah can win this. You said she was in law school, tell her the evidence, she should know. Is she at a good law school?" He asked.

"…Harvard Law", Jennifer answered.

"Well, then she should definitely know", Paul replied.

"No, I can't let my daughter be involved in this mess. I'm sorry", Jennifer said.

The guys looked at each other as they leaned back in their chairs with disappointment etched on their faces. All the hard work that was put into bringing those documents, the people that were killed in order to get those documents, it might turn out to be for nothing. Larry, however, wasn't giving up that easily, he leaned forward towards Jennifer and looked her in the eyes.

"Jennifer, you remember when you came to visit me the first time? You remember what you told me? That you don't blame me for David's death, you blame 'her'? Well this is your chance to get you revenge on 'her', you are not doing this for us, you are doing this for you, for your daughter, and for David as well…it's your retribution Jennifer, it's your family's retribution", Larry said.

Larry's words got through to Jennifer. As far as Jennifer was concerned, Sarah was to blame for destroying her marriage and the death of David. She always wished that Sarah had never gotten into their lives, that things would have been better without Sarah.

"… Okay…when she finishes her semester and comes back I will tell her, I don't want to tell her now and distract her from her studies." Jennifer was persuaded by Larry.

"Fair enough", and Larry accepted her reasons behind delaying telling her daughter now.

The guys breathed a sigh of relief, Larry was smiling, happy that Sarah was gonna get what she deserved. All they had to do now was wait for Bonnie to return so that she could lead the fight to bring down Sarah Phillips. As they were all leaving, Snake made sure he was the last one to leave, and when he did, he did something that he has never done before.

"Goodbye."

Snake was standing next to Larry who was still sitting down, and he looked at Larry and said goodbye. It's something not unusual for a person to say, but Snake has never said that to Larry, and Larry felt that he was saying goodbye for good; that he wasn't going to see him ever again. Snake felt that he had outlived his usefulness, and he had helped Larry to the point that his presence is not needed anymore, and it was finally time for them to part ways.

"Semper Fi", Larry responded as he looked up at the man he saw as his guardian angel.

With a simple pat on the back of Larry's head, Snake turned around and made his way towards the exit. He wasn't just exiting the prison, he was exiting Larry's life as well.

"THANK YOU...FOR EVERYTHING!" Larry yelled out as he was being helped off his chair by the guards. Snake heard Larry, and he stopped and wanted to turn around one last time but he couldn't. He didn't want to look back at someone that meant a lot to him. He always had a soft spot for Larry; that bloodied little 17-year-old in handcuffs. Snake always admired his heart and courage, and he was always by his side like an older brother. Snake, with his head down, didn't turn around, he just smiled, lifted his head, and kept walking out of the prison, and out of Larry's' life.

(phone ringing)

"Sarah Phillips' office, how can I help you?" The secretary answered. "Oh…um OK just one second please", said the secretary as she put the call on hold and called her boss' office. "Excuse me, boss, there is a call on line 1…it's Larry Stone."

Sarah was in her office, busy as usual. She had moved on a long time ago from Larry and thought that their last meeting would have been the end of any contact between them. She was completely immersed now in her empire, and she was taking it from strength to strength, unbeknownst to what Larry was planning this whole time. She was surprised that Larry would be calling her, but she took the call just to see what he wanted.

"Yes", Sarah greeted Larry.

"How are you?" Larry asked.

"Huh, you have never contacted me since you went to prison, and now you call to ask how I'm doing, you don't care about that. You got something to say so go ahead because I'm a busy woman", Sarah told him.

"Touché, I just wanted to call you and tell you that…what goes around comes around", Larry said.

"What's that supposed to mean?" Replied Sarah.

"Well, you have done so much bad shit to people that eventually the tables will turn and something bad will happen to you," Larry explained.

"Are you serious? You are calling to threaten me?! Please, Larry, don't make me laugh", Sarah dismissed his threat.

"You can laugh all you want…oh, by the way, my condolences on the death of your former lover Alan Brennan", Larry said to a stunned Sarah who just opened her mouth, not knowing what to say.

"Take care Sarah… See you soon", Larry hung up the phone.

Sarah took a few seconds before finally putting down the speaker. She never thought she'd hear the name Alan Brennan again. She cut ties with him after he served his purpose and was no longer important. For her, he was just a step towards her reaching the top unlike Alan, who fell in love with her, and that love led him to eventually sacrifice his life in order for her to reach her goal. After putting down the phone, she quickly turned to her computer and searched online for the name Alan Brennan to see if he was really dead. She found a link that led her to a local Miami newspaper that published an obituary for Alan. Sarah didn't know what to think now. She was confused. Whatever mind games Larry was trying to pull on her had worked. Why would Larry mention the death of Alan to her? It couldn't be because of the affair because it has been a few years now and Larry and Sarah are no longer together. She felt that there was some other reason that Larry mentioned Alan's death. She decided to call his brother, Jason's lawyer, to get more information on how he died. But her shock was compounded when Eric's secretary answered the phone and broke the news to Sarah that he was killed in his own home. That news worried Sarah; she just hung up the phone without saying a word. Her heart was beating faster, and she was starting to sweat. Nothing really breaks the stonyhearted Sarah, but alarm bells were now going off in her head; two brothers dead, and Larry calling to offer his condolences on the death of one of those brothers. She laughed when she thought that Larry was threatening her. But she wasn't laughing anymore. Sarah, for the first time in her life, felt threatened. She feared that what Larry meant was that she was next. He killed Jason, then David, the Brennan brothers, and now it was her turn.

"Leaving early today boss?" Her secretary said to Sarah who rushed out of her office. She didn't reply to her. She didn't talk or make eye contact with anyone. She just made her way out of the building, she got in her car and headed home with her two bodyguards escorting her. When she arrived home, her bodyguards would usually wait in the car until told by her to leave. But to their surprise, she called them inside the house. They went in and she was standing waiting for them.

"What am I paying you to do?" she asked them.

Both of them were surprised by that question. "To protect you", they answered.

"That's right...I fear that..." Sarah stops mid-sentence to take a deep breath and compose herself. "I spoke with Larry Stone today, and he threatened to kill me. I believe that he was serious, and I know who he will ask to kill me...I want you to kill him first", Sarah shocked them with her request.

"...Boss, we are not hired killers, we are bodyguards. You are asking us to..." one of them was saying before Sarah interrupted him.

"I am asking you to do your job! You just said that I'm paying you to protect me. Well, killing Larry's bodyguard will protect me", She said.

Her bodyguards had a point in that they weren't killers like Larry's bodyguard. But the reason they were hesitant was because of the target that she is asking them to kill. They know him very well, they know how dangerous he is and they feared to go after him.

"But boss..." Sarah again interrupted them, but this time by slapping them in the face. Her face had gotten red and there was a different look in her eyes; it was fear. Sarah's strong exterior had been broken by Larry's mind games.

"Do your job!" Sarah said while looking them in their eyes. It was the closest that Sarah would ever come to begging, and her bodyguards noticed that she really was in fear for her life.

"…Ok boss", they agreed to hunt and kill Larry's bodyguard before he could harm her.

Sarah remained silent. The words couldn't come out of her mouth, but what she really wanted to say was thank you.

"We will call two other bodyguards to take our place and stay with you 24/7 while we go looking for him. Is there anything else you need boss?" One of them said.

"…No, that's it. You can go", Sarah dismissed them.

The two bodyguards reluctantly began their mission to kill Larry's bodyguard. But their efforts would prove unsuccessful. Sarah, with the replacement bodyguards now patrolling outside her house, decided not to go to work until she hears from her bodyguards that they did their job. Her housemaid was somewhat happy that she's going to be spending all this time at home because she felt sorry for her daughter Allie, who rarely got to see her busy mother. But that wasn't the case, unfortunately for Allie, Sarah spent her time away from her office at work, in her office at home. Even though she was scared for her life, it didn't stop her from getting some work done. A couple of weeks passed and her bodyguards returned from their failed mission.

"Give me some good news," Sarah told them.

"…Boss, Larry's bodyguard…well, we couldn't find him. We asked around and he is pretty notorious, so it's easy to get information on him if you ask the right people. Everybody that we talked to said that he is not in New York anymore. He just disappeared; there is no trace of him. Nobody knows where he went", one of the bodyguards said.

"…Are you sure?" Sarah asked.

"Boss, if Larry did threaten to kill you, I guarantee you that it's not his bodyguard that will do it", he answered.

Sarah remained quiet while trying to recall her conversation with Larry. She was starting to think that maybe she overreacted; perhaps Larry was just messing with her mind, but why? Why after all this time would Larry call her just to mess with her mind? She dismissed her bodyguards and decided to get back to work. Whatever Larry wanted to achieve by that phone call, she didn't want to let it bother her anymore. However, her bodyguards were not as truthful as they seemed. Not only did they find Larry's bodyguard, but they actually had a conversation with him.

They found him standing on the edge of the Hudson River bank, looking into the river with a photo in one hand and his silver gun in the other. The two bodyguards didn't want to alarm him so they called his name. Mark turned around and saw the two men, whom he recognized, standing a clear distance from him. They then put their hands up to show that they were unarmed and they slowly approached him.

"You're a hard man to find", One of them said to Snake.

"Why were you looking for me?" Snake responded.

"Um, we don't want any trouble, we just want to know one thing; were you ordered to kill Sarah?"

"What? Who told you that?" Snake asked.

"Sarah got a call from Larry and she said he threatened her"

"No, she's not on my list", Snake told them.

"Are you sure?" One of them asked.

"You guys know me right?" Snake asked as they both nodded yes. "Then you should know that if I was ordered to kill her then she would be dead already!"

Snake was a straight shooter and is not afraid to speak the truth. He told Sarah's bodyguards to their face that they wouldn't have been able to stop him if he really was ordered to kill her, but he wasn't, and they believed him. But they knew Sarah would not believe it, and she would lose her mind if they told her about their interaction with him, so they decided to lie and tell her that they couldn't find him.

A couple of weeks pass and everything was back to normal and Sarah's little paranoid episode was something she could laugh about now. But, she was just about to discover what Larry meant all along. She just walked into her office in the morning, ready to start another day at work. She saw letters, as usual on her desk waiting for her. She took the letters to check on them when she saw a letter addressed to her personally and not to the company. There was a weird sense of what goes around comes around about this moment; Matt Phillips, Sarah's deceased first husband, went through this exact scenario. It was the divorce letter that he found on his desk that gave him the heart attack that ended his life. The only difference was that Matt sensed what was coming, while Sarah had no idea what was about to hit her. And this time the letter will not end Sarah's life, but it will end her dream. She reached for the letter opener to open the envelope, and she took out the piece of paper that was inside. What she first saw was "Plaintiff, Bonnie Lawrence against, Defendant, Sarah Phillips Stone".

Bonnie Lawrence is back, and she is ready to take what belongs to her.

PART NINETEEN

ALL GROWN UP

19

When Jennifer Lawrence agreed to take Sarah to court, and have her daughter be involved in this situation, she had a stipulation. She demanded that they wait until Bonnie finishes her course and returned home. She didn't want to distract her daughter from her studies. Larry and his lawyer understood her reasoning and agreed to wait.

Bonnie Lawrence was one of the top students at Harvard Law, with a bright future ahead of her. She also happens to be engaged to her long-time boyfriend, who also studied with her at Harvard. After graduating, they plan to open a law firm in Boston. Although they were both New Yorkers, they saw their future in Boston. Bonnie finished the classes that she was taking and was heading back to New York with her fiancé for a short break, not knowing that she was about to be told she is the heir to a multimillion dollar empire that was built by her dad. Her mother picked her up from the airport as usual, and decided to break the news to her about the case with Larry's lawyer present. Jennifer had suggested that they meet at the prison so that Larry can be present as well, but Larry couldn't stand to face the daughter of the man that he had killed. Jennifer reassured him that Bonnie feels the same way as her, and that they both blame Sarah for what happened, but Larry still refused.

"We both forgive you, Larry, I honestly believe that you wouldn't have killed David if it wasn't for HER meddling", Jennifer told Larry on the phone.

"Thank you for your forgiveness. It's something that I couldn't do. But, this isn't my fight Jennifer, it's yours. I'm in your corner but I don't have to be by your side. There is no reason for me to be present. My lawyer

knows all the details, his presence would be enough",
Larry told her.

Jennifer told Paul that Larry declined to meet in prison
and that the meeting will now be at their home. They
arrived back home from the airport and a half hour later,
Paul came over. He was greeted by Jennifer, and led to
the couch in the living room where he made himself
comfortable. Paul was sitting down when he saw Bonnie
coming, and he couldn't help but do a double-take.
Bonnie was the spitting image of Sarah Phillips; from
her natural beauty, her wavy long blonde hair, her
confident strut, all the way down to the fancy business
suit.

"What's going on mom?" Bonnie asked her
mother.

"Sweetie, this is Mr. Paul Beigler...he is Larry
Stone's lawyer, and he is here to talk about something
very important...about your father", Jennifer said.

"...OK", a confused Bonnie said as they all sat
down in the living room.

"...Well, could you tell her Mr. Beigler",
Jennifer asked Paul to explain the situation to Bonnie.

"Sure. How are you, Bonnie?" Paul asked.

"I'm fine, and you? Bonnie replied.

"I'm fine too thanks for asking. Your mother told me that you were already familiar with the details of the case involving Larry Stone", Paul asked her.

"Which details exactly?" she asked.

"…It's…technically this particular detail wasn't a part of the case. It was something that came up after the trial. You know how Sarah took over the company after Larry went to prison?" He said.

"Yeah…" Bonnie said while rolling her eyes at the mention of Sarah's name.

"Now, here's where it gets a little tricky. Larry was never the owner to begin with, so Sarah had no right to take charge of the company. We have discovered the original document of ownership that names Jason Kay as the owner", Paul said.

"Huh…that's the guy that used to work with my dad and later worked for Larry right? The one who overdosed?" Bonnie asked.

"Yes, that's right. After he died, however, his will went missing. And since nobody knew that he was the owner, nobody made an effort to look for Jason's missing will. But we recovered that will in which he names his successor…it was your dad", Paul told her.

"…And my dad is dead, so it belongs to me right? The company's mine?" Bonnie asked.

"…Yes", Said Paul, who was surprised she figured it out before he told her that it was her.

"Hey don't look surprised. Dad became the legal owner because Jason named him his successor in his will. And when he died, my dad's will said nothing about his successor because he didn't know that he was in charge. So since he didn't handpick a successor, legally, the company would go to his kids, and I'm his only child, so it was pretty simple to figure out", Bonnie showed that she already had the mind of a lawyer.

"Honey, you don't have to fight her. It's all up to you, nobody is forcing you to do anything if you don't want to be involved", Jennifer told Bonnie.

"Mom, she was the main reason you and dad broke up. She was probably the reason he was killed too. I'm sorry but you can't say anything that will stop me from going after her. I'm taking what belongs to me", Bonnie was determined to go after Sarah.

Paul was blown away by Bonnie's intelligence and determination; characteristics she inherited from her parents. But it was time to reclaim another inheritance, an empire that was built by her dad.

Sarah had no idea why she was being sued by David's daughter, so she called her lawyer to meet with her urgently. At SP Enterprises, when Sarah calls you, it's the norm to stop whatever it is you were doing and head over to see her. And that's what her lawyer did. He entered her office with the lawsuit in her hand.

"What the hell is this?" Sarah said angrily as she threw the papers at him.

"...Um, we heard about this...for a few days now...someone was planning to sue you. It's David Lawrence's daughter, Bonnie..." her lawyer explained.

"I know who she is! What the hell is she suing me for?!" Sarah asked angrily.

"...She claims to be the rightful owner of this company", said her lawyer.

"...BULLSHIT!! Where does she come off thinking that she owns this company? I AM THIS COMPANY! She wants to start a fight with me, then a fight is what I'm gonna give her", Sarah was never the one to back down from a fight, and she wasn't scared to face Bonnie.

The many twists and turns involving the empire, and all the people who help build it, had now come down to a one on one showdown between Sarah and Bonnie. The two legal teams were preparing for the big trial, as again, news outlets were salivating over a new scandal involving this company. Sarah was led by her lawyer Ethan Ridley, and Bonnie was led by her lawyer Sean Andrews. Sarah's legal team now know that the case is based solely on the two documents that were retrieved;

the original ownership paper and Jason Kay's will in which he confirms that he was the owner and that David was his successor.

"What?! Is that true that Jason was the owner?" Sarah asked her lawyer. It was the first time that she knew about this.

"Yes, that's true", he replied.

"But from where did they get his will? I remember it was stolen", she asked.

"It was stolen, but somehow it magically reappeared", he replied.

"...We should go after the will, right?" Sarah asked him.

"That's the plan; if the will ended up in their hands illegally, or even better if they were the ones who stole it in the first place. Then the judge would have no choice but to throw away that evidence. And without that will, they have no case!" he said.

"Huh, you are finally gonna prove your worth," Sarah said as she smiled at him.

PART TWENTY
EVERYBODY V.S HER

20

(News hosts discussing)

"Now I'm sure you guys heard of this; SP Enterprises, formerly known as JL Enterprises is facing another scandal! Apparently, Sarah Phillips illegally owns the company. Some other woman is suing her for ownership."

"This is ridiculous. I mean, everybody knows that I'm not the biggest Sarah Phillips fan, but you still have to appreciate what she has done after the first scandal. If she loses this, if she goes down, then the company is gonna go down as well. There won't be a recovery from this scandal."

The stage is set; the audience were getting comfortable in their seats, filling the courtroom. The two legal teams were getting a quick few pointers across, as the judge finally entered.

"All rise." The bailiff addressed the courtroom.

Everybody stood up for the entrance of the judge. While they were standing, Sarah looked over at the prosecution table to see Bonnie. She only remembers her when she was a little girl. They only saw each other once before, when Sarah ran into Jennifer and Bonnie at the mall. They only said "hi" to each other, and Sarah had admired how cute Bonnie was. Now the same cute little girl was all grown up. Both women eyed each other with their poker faces, until they were told to take their seats.

"Now, I believe the prosecution only has two pieces of evidence that suggest that Miss Lawrence should be the owner. Correct?" The judge asked.

"Yes your honour", replied Andrews.

"And the defence is arguing against the credibility of this evidence?" The judge asked the defence.

"Yes your honour, we believe that the evidence has illegally ended up in their hands", replied Ridley.

"I'll be the judge of that thank you", the judge said as he gestured with his hand for the prosecution to begin their case.

"Before we begin your honour, I would like to point out that for this trial, we have asked Mr. Paul Beigler, Larry Stone's lawyer, to be present with us on the prosecution table. He played a large role in building our case, and he is the most informed person on this matter", Andrews said.

"Mr. Beigler, I heard you retired?" The judge asked Paul.

"I came back for one last hurrah your honor", Paul replied.

"I don't have a problem with that, any objections, Mr. Ridley?" The judge asked.

"No your honor", Ridley replied.

"Ok, go on", the judge ordered Andrews to continue his opening statement.

"Thank you your honour. The evidence we found clearly states that Mr. Jason Kay was the original owner of the company. When Mr. Beigler found that out, he began to search for the missing will belonging to Jason Kay, in the hopes that it might shed some light on the reason for Jason Kay being named as the owner. The will was found and it states not only the reason for him being named as the owner but also states who should succeed him. That will is the only piece of evidence that we need to legally justify that Bonnie Lawrence is the rightful owner of SP Enterprises", Andrews said.

Ridley got up to deliver his opening remarks.

"Your honor, what Mr. Andrews just said is all the evidence that we need. How can a will that was reported as stolen by Jason Kay's lawyer just be found after almost 4 years? How can evidence that reeks of some sort of foul play being involved in the retrieval of it be presented in court? Your honour, I ask you to throw away that evidence if no foul play can be proven", Ridley replied.

"In that case, the defence should go first", the judge said.

"Thank you your honour. The defence would like to call Mr. Paul Beigler to the stand", Ridley said.

Paul knew that he was going to be called, and he confidently got up to go to the stand.

"Raise your right hand. Do you swear to tell the truth, the whole truth and nothing but the truth so help you God?"

"I do," Beigler said.

Paul Beigler took his seat on the witness stand, ready to be questioned about the will.

"Could you state for the court who you are."

"I'm Paul Beigler, Larry Stone's lawyer."

"How long have you been Larry's lawyer?"

"Well I was his father's lawyer, and after he passed away, I decided to stay on and be Larry's lawyer, so over ten years."

"So you could say that there is more than just a professional relationship between you and Mr. Stone since you two go way back?"

"I guess you could say that, yes. I think all of his dad's acquaintances who saw him go through his parents' death felt a close bond with him after that."

"So was that bond close in which you would do 'anything' to help him?"

"Objection your honour, he is trying to suggest that Mr. Beigler has done something illegal", Andrews interrupted.

"Sustained. Mr. Ridley, if you have a particular question to ask, go ahead and ask it straight out, no need to go in circles", the judge told Ridley.

"Mr. Beigler, how did Jason Kay's will end up in your hands?"

"…Well, I wanted to look for Mr. Kay's will after I found a copy of the ownership documents that had his signature as owner…"

"That's not what I asked. I asked how it ended up in your hands; not why you wanted to look for it."

"…I asked for help from Larry Stone's bodyguard to look for it. He found it with a certain Alan Brennan, the older brother of Eric Brennan, Jason Kay's lawyer."

"And where are they now, the Brennan brothers? Could they come to testify in this court?"

"…No."

"And why is that?

"They are dead."

"Two brothers dead in the space of a few months and then the will ends up in your hands."

Beigler didn't say anything.

"No more questions your honour."

Ridley was done questioning him. Andrews quickly got up and began questioning Paul Beigler.

"Mr. Beigler, did you kill Eric Brennan"

"No, I didn't."

"Did you kill Alan Brennan?"

"No, I didn't."

"Did you order someone to kill them?"

"No, I didn't."

"Did you steal the will from them?"

"No, I didn't."

"Thank you Mr. Beigler. No more questions your honour." Andrews kept his questions simple and straight to the point.

The first duel saw Ridley suggest to the judge that because of the close relationship between Larry and his lawyer, he would go to any measures to protect him, even if it was illegal. But it was deflected well by Andrews who asked Beigler straight questions in which, he denied killing them and stealing the will from them.

"The defence would like to call Sarah Phillips to the stand." Ridley called Sarah to begin questioning her.

"Mrs. Phillips, when did you find out that Jason Kay was supposedly the original owner?"

"Last week, when we were preparing for this trial."

"Mr. Kay never told you about this?"

"No, he never said anything about it."

"What did you do after Larry Stone went to jail, in terms of taking control of the company?"

"Well, there was nothing that I was supposed to do, since I was the wife of who I believed at the time to be the owner, I became the legal owner after he went to prison."

"Your honour, Sarah Phillips, the true owner of the company took charge legally after her husband went to prison. She didn't do anything wrong, it's a shame that she has to be taken to court after all the hard work that she put into the company", Ridley finished questioning Sarah.

"Mrs. Phillips, you worked with Mr. Kay before working together with Larry Stone, is that correct?" Andrews began questioning her.

"Yes, that's correct."

"And how would you describe your relationship with Jason Kay?"

"Objection your honour, irrelevant to the case", Ridley interrupted..

"Your honour, if there was no close relationship between Mrs. Phillips and Mr. Kay, then he probably wouldn't have disclosed to her the secret that he was in charge", Andrews explained.

"Overruled. Answer the question Mrs. Phillips", the judge said.

"…What would you define as close? I worked with the man for over ten years", Sarah told Andrews.

"I mean would you two hang out after work, go to the movies, stuff like that. Or was it just a professional relationship where you just saw each other at work?" Andrews asked.

"…If we went by your definition, then no, we didn't have a close relationship!" Truth was, they did have a somewhat close relationship but Jason never trusted her enough to tell her that he was the owner.

"No more questions your honour."

The court was adjourned and was to resume after two days. The defence was the happiest with the proceedings of the first day. The prosecution team met to discuss their strategy.

"Did that bodyguard kill the Brennan brothers?" Andrews asked Beigler.

"I honestly don't know, I heard that one of them was shot and the other was an accident", replied Beigler.

"Then we need to get the coroner's report for Alan and Eric Brennan to prove that their deaths weren't related. They want to call Larry Stone to the stand, let's hope he doesn't know too much about what his bodyguard did or didn't do", Andrews said.

"Will that be enough? Proving that their deaths weren't related?" Bonnie asked.

"No. We still need to prove without using Jason's will that he was the owner", Andrews replied.

"Shouldn't we contact people who worked with Jason at JL Enterprises?" Bonnie asked.

"Yeah, I already got the list of the former board members who came with Jason and Sarah, perhaps one of them was in on it too, and maybe Jason told one of them he was the owner", replied Andrews. But those board members never knew about Jason's secret identity, and they declined to come to the trial. They moved on to other jobs after being fired by Sarah, and could care less about what was going on in this trial.

After hearing about the trial in the news, Judy Nichols contacted Sarah to offer to babysit her daughter Allie. She figured with her being preoccupied with the trial, she could use some help taking care of Allie. Judy was a kind-hearted person, even with all the personal animosity between Sarah and Larry, she still made the effort to visit Sarah in the hospital when she gave birth, and remained in contact with her after that. Sarah knew she was a good person, and that she did have a point, so she told the housemaid to take Allie to her aunt and uncle's to stay there for a while until she is done with the trial, for she was confident of winning. The two legal teams were ready to resume the proceedings of the trial. The judge came in and everybody was seated.

"Your honour, the defence would like to call Larry Stone to the stand," Ridley informed the judge.

The courtroom became silent as Larry made his emerged through the courtroom doors. He was escorted by his arms, and his hands were handcuffed. He was led by his arms to the stand where he took his seat; he sat there, and looked over at the prosecution table and smiled at Paul. As his eyes glanced over, he saw Bonnie for the first time and he didn't know what facial expression to convey to her, whether to smile or look away. The smile went away and he just had a confused stare, but Bonnie smiled back at him. What was surprising was that he didn't even try to look over at Sarah, who herself wasn't looking at Larry, as if they were two people who have never met.

"Now before we begin, where is this bodyguard who found the will? He is mentioned a lot and seems to be a key character in this case, why isn't he on the list to testify?" The judge asked.

"He is dead your honour! We have his death certificate here, he was shot twice in the chest two weeks ago", replied Andrews.

"Hmm, what a shame. If he was still alive he would just testify if he stole it or not, that would have saved us some time", the judge said as he quickly looked at the death certificate and handed it back to the bailiff.

Paul looked over at Larry on the stand to see his reaction. Larry was staggered by the news of Mark's death. He was looking around at everyone, panicked and confused, wanting to get more information on how and when this happened. His eyes were starting to water, and he was biting his lips. He raised his handcuffed hands like a schoolboy in class would, to get permission to see the death certificate. The look of despair on Larry's face convinced the judge to allow Larry to look at the certificate.

The bailiff went over to hand Larry the paper. Holding the certificate in one hand, he looked at it to get confirmation that his older brother was indeed dead! He dropped the paper, which fell from the stand and landed on the courtroom floor, as he put his head in his hands. The judge gave him a minute before he spoke to him.

"Mr. Stone, can you continue?" The judge asked him.

After taking a deep breath, Larry responded.

"...Yeah...lets just get this over with."

Larry composed himself, and was ready to be grilled by the defence. The fate of the trial now rests on whether Larry knew that his late bodyguard had killed the Brennan brothers.

"Could you state who you are please." Ridley was up to begin questioning Larry.

"I'm Larry Stone."

"Larry Stone, the former owner of SP Enterprises?"

"Yes, I'm the former owner of JL Enterprises." Larry made sure to refer to the company in the name that he gave it.

"Could you tell us a little about your recently departed bodyguard?"

"His name was Mark Nichols, a retired Marine, and the eldest child of my dad's friend. He worked at his dad's security company. I then hired him to be my bodyguard."

"Did you ever ask your bodyguard to do anything else besides protecting you? Something that a regular bodyguard wouldn't do?"

Larry took his time trying to find a way to answer this question. The prosecution team, as well as Paul Beigler, held their breath, awaiting Larry's answer.

"Could you answer the question Mr. Stone", the judge told Larry.

"…No, I didn't", Larry finally answered.

"You took some time to answer that question, why is that?" Ridley asked.

"I have known the guy for more than 10 years, I can't recall 10 years worth of conversations in just a few seconds. I needed some time to remember if I did or did not."

"Your bodyguard was the one who finally found the will, right? Where did he find it?"

"Yes, it was with Alan Brennan. He was the one who stole it in the first place; he was protecting Mrs. Phillips because the two of them were having an affair while she was married to me."

"There is no need to divulge into her personal life."

Even though Larry never knew about the affair until he was recently told about it by Mark, it was not the best kept secret within JL Enterprises. There were a few employees who knew, and that was the reason why

Larry acknowledging it was not suspicious to those in the courtroom.

"First you say that I take too long to answer and now you don't like how I answer. Why did you call me to the stand if I can't answer the way I want to? If you don't like how I answer then just give me yes or no questions."

"Alright, I'll give you yes or no questions. Did your bodyguard kill Alan Brennan?"

"I don't know!"

"Did he kill Eric Brennan?" With each question he asked, Ridley's voice kept getting louder and louder, as he was moving closer to Larry on the stand.

"I don't know!" Larry answered.

"Was your bodyguard capable of killing Alan Brennan and Eric Brennan?" Ridley asked.

"OBJECTION your honour!! The question is ambiguous; the guy was a 6 foot 2 bodyguard and former Marine, of course he was CAPABLE of killing someone, it doesn't prove that he did!" Andrews quickly jumped in.

"Sustained. It's right Mr. Ridley, just because he was able, it doesn't prove that he did", the judge agreed with Andrews' objection.

"…Did he kill Jason Kay?" Ridley asked.

"Objection your honour! How Jason Kay died is irrelevant to this case. Besides, the police ruled it as a drug overdose. So he can't go around screaming murder without any proof", Andrews jumped in again.

"Sustained. You are treading a fine line Mr. Ridley. If you don't have any proof to back your questions then I suggest you change the subject", warned the judge.

"No more questions your honour", Ridley felt a little frustrated that Larry didn't confess to the illegal dirty work that he had ordered his bodyguard to do.

"Your honour, before I begin questioning Mr. Stone, I would like to present the coroner's and the police's report concerning the deaths of both Eric and Alan Brennan. While Eric Brennan was shot and killed in his home and the case is still unsolved, Alan Brennan's case is closed, your honour. The coroner found alcohol in his body three times the legal limit. The police ruled that his death was an accident…he fell down the stairs. Your honour, this police report should stop the defence from inferring that Mr. Stone or his bodyguard were involved with his death. It should also rule out that there is any relation between their deaths", Andrews said.

"The police report will be taken into account. Proceed with your questions", the judge ordered.

"Mr. Stone, when were you made aware that Jason Kay was the owner of the company?"

"About 6 months ago."

"Did you know why he named himself the owner?"

"Objection your honour, he is calling to mention a fact that is in the evidence which has not yet been presented in court."

"Sustained. Would you like to rephrase your question Mr. Andrews?" The judge asked.

"No. I actually have no more questions for Mr. Stone", Andrews said.

The court was adjourned and they had a couple of days to regroup. Sarah was feeling that she was losing this case. She had to go on the offensive in order protect her empire. Sarah was sitting down next to Ridley and she was shaking her head in frustration. She puffed her cheeks and was looking around the meeting room to make sure no one can hear her even though it was just the two of them, and she shared new information with Ridley

"I think I can prove that Larry used his bodyguard to do his dirty work as well," Sarah told Ridley.

"What do you mean? How can you prove that?" Ridley replied.

"...I know he killed Jason Kay, I was next to him when he made the call to his bodyguard", Sarah confessed. Her lawyer didn't know how to respond to this revelation.

"Put me on the stand again," Sarah told him.

"...Is that all there is? Or is there more to this that you are not telling me?" Ridley asked.

"What do you mean?" Sarah asked.

"This information can be used against you. Jason's death would be changed for an OD to murder, and you could be charged with aiding and abetting if you knew that Larry ordered his bodyguard to kill Jason and you didn't stop him. But it's best that I don't know all the details. It's your decision if you wanna go through with this", Ridley told her.

Sarah was thinking about this long and hard. Her lawyer was right; she would put herself in a sticky situation if she reveals this information to the court.

"...If I'm going down. I'm going down fighting", But Sarah, as always, was determined to go through with her plan, and she wasn't gonna back down.

"Okay then. How many days after the call was Jason killed?" he asked.

"…I think the next day, I can't remember clearly", Sarah replied.

"We need to get Jason's death certificate to be certain. We also need to get the phone record for Larry's phone", Ridley said.

"His phone was registered to the company so it's easy to get that," Sarah replied.

Their plan to go on the offensive was picking up steam. As they went in the court again, the opposing legal team had no idea what they were planning.

"Your honour, I would like to call Sarah Phillips to the stand again," Ridley said.

"Okay go ahead", the judge told them.

Sarah made her way to the stand, but without her usual confident strut, she was nervously looking down.

"Your honour, Jason Kay's death was brought up before but it was immediately shot down as it was judged as irrelevant to the case. But after further discussion with my client, I realized that his death proves that Larry had used his bodyguard for illegal tasks", Ridley explained.

Larry, who was in the courtroom again, was shocked at this new plan as he furrowed his eyebrows. Bonnie and her table looked at each other with a confused look because they didn't know what was going on.

"Mrs. Phillips, would you like to share with us how Jason Kay died?" Ridley asked Sarah.

"…Well, I will go back to the time before he died. We were having a meeting and things got heated between Larry and Jason. Jason provoked Larry to fire him but Larry replied that he wasn't going to fire him, that it would be too easy. That was the last thing he ever said to him. Later that night, Jason called me, scared for his life, wanting to find out from me what Larry meant. After I hung up the phone, Larry left the room with his phone for just a few seconds. After he went to sleep I checked who he called, and it was his bodyguard…the very next day, Jason Kay was dead", Sarah said.

"Your honour, we have the phone records here to back what my client is saying. Her phone records show that she did receive a call from Mr. Jason Kay a day before he died, and that Larry made a call a few minutes after that call. And now we want to call Larry Stone again to the witness stand to clarify if that person that he called was his bodyguard", Ridley said.

Bonnie and her lawyer didn't know what to expect as they were unfamiliar with Larry's history. Sarah was leaving the witness stand, with her heart was pumping fast, and she was sweating profusely. She wasn't her usual confident self because she just put herself out there to be taken down. If Larry confesses to killing Jason, then Sarah might be in trouble now that she confessed she knew Larry called his bodyguard to order the hit. She just handed Larry a double-edged sword. Now she had to wait and see if Larry was going to take a stab at her, because if he does, he will be taking not just himself out, but Sarah as well. Larry was seated on the stand, and the fate of this case now rests on what he has to say.

"Mr. Stone, is this phone record correct? Do you remember that you made a call after Sarah talked to Jason that night?" Ridley asked.

"...Yes I do."

"Do you recall that it lasted only 22 seconds?"

"...Yes I do."

"May I ask who you called for just 22 seconds on that night, a day before Mr. Kay died?"

"...My bodyguard...I called my bodyguard."

"Your bodyguard...who I should point out goes by the nickname Snake. So what was that short conversation with 'Snake' about?"

"Objection your honour, Mr. Stone doesn't have to give details of a private conversation," Andrews said. He knew his objection was not merited, but he was just buying Larry some time to think of a good way to answer.

"This private conversation is now very important to this case...Overruled. Answer the question Mr. Stone", the judge said.

"I can't remember," Larry said.

"You can recall that it lasted 22 seconds but you can't remember what it was about?!" Ridley asked sarcastically.

Larry, with his back against the ropes, now had to think of a good way to respond to that thorny question; otherwise, he could cost this case for Bonnie.

"Mr. Stone, we are still awaiting an answer", the judge told him. But Larry remained quiet.

"Okay, I will try to refresh your memory. Did you tell him to kill Jason Kay?" Ridley directly asked him.

Larry didn't know what to say. Paul looked over at Andrews and shook his head as if to say it's over, Larry was cornered and wasn't going to be able to get out of this. Concern was also present at the defence table where Sarah was sitting. She felt that her plan was working, Larry was gonna confess, but that also meant that she might be in trouble now.

"Did you TELL HIM TO KILL JASON KAY?!" Ridley shouted at him.

Ridley was now getting angry at Larry's continued silence, and he raised his voice as he asked him again. Then the most surprising thing happened; a grin, the same evil grin that Larry would always get when he is about to do something sinister, was drawn on his face. He had finally thought of a way out.

"…I can tell you what my exact words were..." Larry finally answered.

" Fantastic!" Ridley sarcastically responded. "Would you like to share with us what these words were?"

"…Yes…if you do me a favour?"

"What? What favour could I possibly offer you?"

"You have my phone records with you right? Could you look over it and tell me how many other times I called my bodyguard", Larry asked Ridley who was confused by this favour. He had Larry's phone record in his hands and was looking over it.

"I can tell you that you will only find one other phone call made to that number, but you have to go a bit far back to find that call. It also was a short conversation", Larry said.

"I'm interested to see where you are going with this. Is what Mr. Stone saying true?" The judge asked Ridley who was still looking over the paper.

"…Umm…yeah, there's just one other phone call made to this number. It lasted just over a minute", Ridley confirmed that what Larry was saying was true.

"Thank you, now I will tell you what those two conversations with Snake were about," Larry had created a suspense filled courtroom. You could hear a pin drop as everyone was quiet and on the edge of their seats, waiting to hear what Larry was gonna say.

"They were of course to my bodyguard. The first phone call was concerning a rich businessman who wanted to rival us in the city. We were still growing as a company and we wouldn't have been able to compete with him. I first asked her and Jason to go deal with him and try to convince him perhaps to change his plans. She was there, she can confirm that what I'm saying is true", Larry said as he pointed at Sarah, "but they failed to do that. So I asked my bodyguard to 'take care' of the guy. It was mentioned before that my bodyguard was a former marine. Do you know what his role was in the Marines?" Larry asked Ridley who nodded his head no. "He was an interrogator, and he was the best in persuasion and extraction of information, and I can say that from personal experience. So I thought I would use his persuasion skills on this businessman…and that businessman didn't die, did he? To be honest, I have no idea what he did to him. He convinced him to change his plans, I don't know how, but he didn't kill him. Hell, the businessman didn't even come after us. He was rich and powerful, he could have sued us or I don't know, done something to us if my bodyguard had done something illegal, but he didn't! Now the second phone call, I told him to 'take care' of Jason Kay, those were my exact words, the same words I told him when I wanted him to persuade the businessman. Anybody who knew Jason knew that he was a stubborn, arrogant, and downright confusing guy. I mean, on the weekends, the guy would be like a kid who just wanted to party, and when it was time for serious business, he would turn into the smartest guy in the room. You never knew what to expect with him. He was actually threatening me, his boss, to fire him. I knew that he wasn't gonna leave that easily even if I fired him, that's why I told my bodyguard. Jason had a history with drugs, she can back this up as well", again pointing at Sarah, "you can look over his death certificate, it was ruled a drug overdose, the police found no evidence of foul play. Maybe our dispute during the meeting caused him to overindulge in his drug use. Or perhaps the phone call between him and Sarah the night before he died did the trick. Or perhaps my bodyguard scared him into overdosing. The only way to find out if my bodyguard was involved is if he takes the stand…but he's not here. So, can YOU prove which of these theories is true? You can't! Because without definitive proof, they are just theories", Larry ended his long speech that stunned the entire courtroom.

He completely smashed Sarah's offensive in a way nobody expected. His bodyguard was no amateur; he never did give Larry details of what he does or how he does it, in order to protect Larry from knowing too much. He was the one that decided to have a separate phone number just for Larry to call. And he told him to always keep the call short and straight to the point. So technically, Larry was telling the truth.

"I told you all I know. Can I leave now? And if you believe that what I just said was all lies, you have a witness sitting right there, go ahead and call her again to the stand", Larry said to a stunned Ridley, who in a low voice said that he had no more questions as he retreated back to his table. With that, Larry metaphorically dropped the microphone as he was escorted off the stand. But Larry wasn't done with Sarah. As he left the stand, he stuck out his handcuffed arms and gestured for Sarah to take the stand and rebuke what he just said in the same way that a matador, holding the red cape would gracefully gesture for the bull to charge. It was an arrogant and somewhat unnecessary move from Larry. He was just pouring salt onto the wounded Sarah. But Sarah, just like the bull would do, took the bait and charged at Larry.

"YOU'RE LYING! You killed Jason! I know you did!" Sarah got out of her chair and started yelling at Larry.

"Order!" The judge said, hitting his gavel.

"You know what; I wish you had been with your parents that night, so I could have watched YOU DIE

WITH THEM!!" Sarah had completely lost it. She was now being held back by Ridley.

"ORDER!" The judge yelled louder as he smacked his gavel twice, as hard as he could. Gasps filled the courtroom after what Sarah just said, and even Larry was in shock at what Sarah just said to him.

Larry felt hurt by what she just said. He wanted to retaliate but he felt that he had done enough. He had broken Sarah; all he had to do now was sit back and enjoy Sarah's demise. Ridley was now whispering in Sarah's ear asking her to calm down. She took a couple of deep breaths and she did calm down, as Ridley helped her sit back down.

"Mr. Ridley, if your client wishes to reply to Mr. Stone, all she has to do is take the stand again", the judge warned Ridley.

"I know your honour, I apologize on behalf of my client", Ridley replied.

"Does she wish to reply in an orderly manner?" The judge asked.

"No, your honour." Ridley didn't even ask Sarah, he made the decision not to send her to the stand again based on the fact that she clearly wasn't in the right state of mind.

"Okay…I will give you both some time to deliberate…this court is in recess." The judge told the two legal teams as he got up and left to his chambers.

The two legal teams regrouped to discuss the state of the case after Larry's stunning speech. Sarah and her team felt like they had just hit a road block. They based their entire defence around the fact that Larry used his bodyguard to do illegal deeds, but that was shot down by Larry, who was right in saying there was no proof of that.

"I'm sorry." Sarah apologized to her lawyer for her outburst.

"Just forget about it, we need to change our defence, there just isn't enough evidence. Unless…that businessman that Larry said his bodyguard scared away…maybe if we can find him, he can come testify to what the bodyguard did", Ridley said.

"Will that work?" Sarah asked.

"…Only if, for example, he threatened him with a gun or something, if not then his testimony will just backfire on us", Ridley explained. The team continued to discuss what strategy they would take next. While they were doing that, Bonnie and her team were having a similar discussion about their next move in another meeting room.

"What the hell just happened?" Andrews asked Beigler.

"That's Larry Stone for you. Nobody should underestimate him", Beigler chuckled.

"Was it all true? All that stuff about his bodyguard?" Andrews asked.

"Well..." Beigler was about to explain.

"On second thought, don't answer that. I don't wanna know! We should just be happy that it went in our favour. Larry just put them in a corner, we just need to deliver the knockout blow now", Andrews said.

"How are we gonna do that?" Bonnie asked him.

As the team was discussing their next steps, Paul Beigler's phone began to ring. He took it out of his pocket, looked at the screen but it was a number he didn't recognize.

"Yes?" Beigler answered the phone. "I'm sorry, Jeremy who?" Beigler said as he decided to leave the room so that he can have some privacy. He returned after a few minutes with a Larry-esque grin on his face.

"Do you have any suggestions Mr. Beigler?" Bonnie asked.

"...We got this, the case is yours Bonnie", Paul answered her as he was still holding his phone in his hand. The phone call that he got, from a person he had never met before, was the exact knockout blow that Andrews was looking for.

"And how will that happen?" Andrews asked.

"We can prove that Jason was the owner without using the will. There's not much time left til we go back to the courtroom...he is on his way", Paul explained.

"Who's he?" Andrews questioned.

Paul quickly explained to them what happened in the phone call, and who the person on the other end was. When they went back to the courtroom, Beigler informed the judge that they have a last minute witness that they want to call to the stand.

"I see this person wasn't in the original list of people to testify", the judge observed.

"No your honour, we were contacted by this individual recently", Beigler explained.

"Well, you do know that the defence will also have their chance to question him," the judge said.

"Yes, your honour", Beigler replied.

"Okay then, go ahead", the judge allowed Beigler to call his witness.

"Your honour, the prosecution would like to call Jeremy Kay to the stand," Beigler said.

Jason Kay's twin brother was the one who called Paul Beigler, he saw the trial on the news, and heard about how they found Jason's missing will. He wanted to know the contents of the will, and Paul Beigler agreed to tell him if he would testify as to why he wants to know the contents of the will.

"Could you state who you are for the court please", Beigler got up this time and began with his questions.

"I'm Jeremy Kay, Jason Kay's brother, isn't it obvious?" Jeremy joked. It was apparent to everyone in the courtroom who knew Jason that the childish sense of humour runs in the family.

"Mr. Kay, you contacted us because you wanted to know the contents of your brothers will, correct?"

"Yes, I was looking really hard after his death for that will, but our lawyer said it was stolen. I couldn't find it anywhere."

"You and Jason had the same lawyer?"

"Yes, Eric Brennan was our lawyer."

"And you both made your wills with him?"

"Yes, we were together when we made our wills with Eric."

"Did your will go missing as well?"

"No, that's what was strange about it, of all the clients that he had, only Jason's will went missing. That's why we all assumed it was stolen."

"Now, Mr. Kay, is there any particular reason why you were so vigorously searching, why you were the only one in fact, searching for Jason Kay's will besides the reason that he was your brother?"

"…Yes… Jason told me that he was the owner of JL Enterprises. I was hoping that maybe he left the company to me. I know it sounds stupid, it was a long shot but there were millions of dollars at stake, you know, so I had to try my luck and see if he left it to me."

Jason was disappointed with the fact that he was the owner but David told him to keep it a secret. It was an itch that he needed to scratch, so he told his brother about it. Thanks to Jason Kay's big mouth, Beigler believed that they had done enough for the judge to take Jason's will into consideration. Beigler smiled, and he was done questioning Jeremy, but to everyone's surprise, Jeremy had a question for Paul.

"I wanted to ask you over the phone but I forgot; were you named after Paul Beigler, the lawyer from that movie?"

"What?" Paul was bemused by that question, and so was the judge.

"Mr. Kay, we have more pressing issues to address", the judge told Jeremy.

"Yeah but don't you think it's weird that there was a lawyer named Paul Beigler in a movie, and standing in front of us is Paul Beigler, a lawyer in real life!" Jeremy turned to speak to the judge, who began rubbing his forehead in frustration at Jeremy's extraneous issue.

"I was not named after that character, and it was a coincidence that I became a lawyer as well!" Paul answered him just to shut him up, and he sat back down.

"I thought so, because you look nothing like Jimmy Stewart!" Jeremy said.

"Ridley, could you please...?" The judge motioned for Ridley to quickly get up and begin questioning Jeremy in order to shut him up.

"Mr. Kay, it was you that contacted the prosecution correct?"

"Yes I searched for Paul Beigler's number and I called him."

"You just did that out of your own free will?"

"Yes, I already said because I wanted to know what was in Jason's will."

"Were you offered anything in return to come and testify?"

"Objection your honour, he is inferring some sort of bribery was involved without any substantial evidence", Andrews interrupted.

"Your honour, Mr. Jeremy Kay's brother died and all that he was worried about was what will happen to the multi-million dollar company, he obviously values money. Who's to say he wasn't given any to come and testify?"

"Overruled", the judge said.

"Now I will ask again, were you offered anything to come and testify?" Ridley asked again.

"Yes, they told me they will tell me the contents of the will. That's all I wanted. I didn't take any money from anyone to come here!" Jeremy explained.

Realizing that he was at a dead end, Ridley had no questions for Jeremy Kay. He sat back down and Jeremy stepped down from the stand, who himself didn't have any more questions of his own, which was a relief to the judge. The judge had already made a decision in his mind in terms of allowing Jason's will to be presented in court, and Jeremy Kay's testimony just cemented what he already had in mind. Jason's will has served as an untouched holy grail so far, but the judge will now decide whether its content will be revealed.

"The testimony of Mr. Jeremy Kay, proving that Jason was the owner, along with the failure of the defence to provide significant evidence that Mr. Stone used his bodyguard, or Marine, whatever you would like to call him, as a henchman to do his dirty work, is enough for me to allow you Mr. Andrews, to present your evidence to the court", the judge made his decision to allow them to present the will, much to the delight of Bonnie and her team.

Andrews got up with the will in his hand, as Bonnie looked over at Sarah with her head down, knowing that this could be the end for her.

"Your honour, this is Jason Kay's last will and testament. I would like to read the inheritance part of the will", Andrews said.

"I, Jason Fisher Kay, leave my car and beach house to my brother..."

"Pfft, I already took those." Jeremy Kay whispered to himself.

"As for JL Enterprises, I was entrusted to be the owner of the company since Larry was too young...but if you are reading this will then it means I'm dead, and I have the power to name my successor...my successor should be David Lawrence. He was the architect behind the success of JL Enterprises, and he trusted me to be the owner, but I turned my back on him. So I am giving him what rightfully belongs to him."

Andrews finished reading the will and Sarah had her head down the whole time.

"Your honour, this will states that David Lawrence was named as the owner after Jason Kay's death. Since David didn't know about this, he didn't name a successor. So by law, the company would be inherited by his children. Your honour, Bonnie Lawrence is the only child of David Lawrence. It's simple, the company belongs to Bonnie Lawrence. Not only that, but the fact that there have been only two owners to JL Enterprises, Mr. Kay and Mr. Lawrence, both of whom have no relation to Mrs. Phillips, it means not only does Mrs. Phillips have no right to own this company, but no right to even fight for something that was never hers or her husband's", Andrews folded the will as he sat back down.

"Mr. Ridley, any rebuttals?" The judge asked Ridley.

Sarah stood up instead, as her lawyer looked at her; he wasn't planning for her to speak. But she whispered to him that she wanted to say something.

"Your honour, my client wishes to say something", Ridley told the judge.

"As long as you keep it civil this time, go ahead Mrs. Phillips", the judge said.

"Your honour, I took charge of this company after my husband went to jail. What I did in four years is more than what he, Jason, or David did in 10 years. Just look at the news, listen to what everybody is saying. This company would be nothing without me. Only I was strong enough to turn around the fortunes of this company after the mess that he put it through", Sarah said as she pointed at Larry. "If I'm not in charge, then there will be no SP Enterprises. And I did nothing illegal for it to be taken away from me", Sarah sat back down, only to notice Bonnie standing up ready to say something.

"Your honour, my client wishes to say something", Andrews told the judge.

"Well it seems only fair since we just heard from Mrs. Phillips. Go ahead Miss Lawrence", the judge said.

"Your honour, I agree with what Mrs. Phillips just said. I follow the news and I hear about all the great things that she has done for the company. Nobody can deny that she has done exceptionally well not just in turning around the fortunes of the company, but in taking it to new heights. And she is right in saying that the company will be nothing without her, nobody can follow what she has done. That's why, if I get the company, my first action would be to dissolve it. I don't have many memories of my father, but the thing that I always remember him saying is you have the whole world in front of you, you can be anything you want, if you believe in yourself, if you follow your heart and work hard enough, then you can live your dream. I'm not a businesswoman, I'm a lawyer or at least I'm hoping to be. I believe that I would be honouring my dad by not taking charge and ending the company that he built so I can follow my dream of being a lawyer. I now address my words directly to you." Bonnie said as she turned and faced Sarah, who was looking up at her, not knowing what she was going to say to her. "I just want you to know that me and my mom don't blame Larry for what happened to my dad, we blame you. If there is one person that can be blamed for all the misfortune that the people around you endured, it would be you." Bonnie said as she sat back down. Everyone had their say in this case. The only thing left was for the judge to deliver his ruling.

"Well, I must say that I'm a little sad that this case has come to an end. In my 30 years as a judge, I have never presided over a trial with as many, let's say, unique individuals. The funny thing is that perhaps the two most interesting individuals involved in this case; Mr. Jason Kay and this snake bodyguard, weren't present for the trial. I would have loved to see what they would have said. Anyway, I'm digressing, I'm sure you want to hear my verdict instead. The prosecution built their case around Jason Kay's will. That will along with the failure of the defence to provide any evidence of foul play in the retrieval of that will is sufficient enough for me to rule that by the letter of the law, the company should be in the hands of Miss Bonnie Lawrence. Case dismissed." The judge ended the trial.

Jubilation erupted at the prosecution table as the judge hit his gavel to end the case, and hammer the final nail into Sarah's coffin. Bonnie jumped up and hugged her mother and fiancé who were sitting behind her. Paul Beigler shook hands with Sean Andrews and congratulated him on a job well done. Larry stood up and smiled at Beigler, but it was also time to escort him back to his jail cell. As he walked past Sarah with an expressionless look on her face, he just smiled at her. The case was over, and so was JL/SP Enterprises.

The following day, Bonnie went to the company to inform everyone that the company will be liquidated. Since a lot of people were going to lose their jobs, Bonnie gave them priority to be hired should they want to work for her when she opens her law firm.

Jennifer Lawrence spoke to Larry and told him that she was going to visit him in prison to personally thank him for helping in the case. Paul was already there with his now former client. But what Jennifer didn't tell Larry was that Bonnie and her fiancé were accompanying her. They arrived at the prison, Jennifer entered and Larry stood up, but was shocked to see Bonnie walking behind her. Larry stood still as Bonnie walked towards Larry and stood face to face with him.

"Larry…" Bonnie said as she faced her dad's killer for the first time.

Larry still didn't know what to say to her, and he remained quiet, as he struggled to maintain eye contact with her.

"I wanted to come so that I can personally thank you. It was all because of you and Mr. Beigler that we were able to win the case", Bonnie said.

Larry was still silent.

"Larry, I know that my dad killed your parents, and for that I apologize. But if you feel that you took away my dad too, you didn't. I lost my dad when I was 7 years old, not when you killed him. After my mom and dad divorced, I stayed with my mom and I never saw my dad again. You weren't responsible for my parents' divorce, Sarah was. You could at least say you're welcome." Bonnie was trying her best to convince Larry that she does not have any animosity towards him.

"…You're welcome." Larry finally responded.

"So what are you planning to do with your inheritance?" Asked Paul.

"Well, I can't think about that now. I still want to focus on my studies, and after I finish I will see what lies ahead. But I do know that me and my fiancé can have a nice honeymoon now. He wanted to go to

Mexico but I think we can afford to go somewhere more extravagant now", Bonnie said.

"…Maldives is nice. You should think about going there", Larry told them.

"We will think about that." Bonnie replied with a smile.

"I am up for parole in 15 year and…um." Larry wanted to ask her for help in making him a free man again, but she interrupted him before he can finish.

"Sure, I will be here", Bonnie agreed to help him without letting him even ask.

With Paul Beigler having officially retired now, Bonnie accepted to represent Larry when he is up for parole. The crazy and unexpected events that happened in their lives has now culminated in the forming of the unlikeliest partnership. Bonnie left the prison and like her dad used to tell her, now had her whole life ahead of her, only now she has a few million dollars in her pocket. Paul Beigler however, stayed after they left. And he was shaking his head and smiling at Larry.

"What is it?" Larry asked him

"I just realized something; you lied under oath! When you said 'take care' of Jason, you did mean to kill him didn't you?" Paul asked.

"Technically I didn't, he just asked me what I said, but he never asked me what I meant did he? Snake always told me to keep the conversation short, so I got lucky the two times I ordered him to do something, I used the same phrase. The first time I really just wanted him to threaten that guy, and the second time, I wanted him to kill!" Larry said.

"So he did kill Jason? But how did he know that you wanted him to kill the second time around?" Paul asked.

"Snake hated Jason, I'm sure he was all too happy to interpret what I said as an order to kill." Larry laughed.

"That was a very risky move to admit in court what you actually said to your bodyguard. I mean, how would you know that Ridley wouldn't ask what you meant?" Beigler asked.

"Mind games my friend, mind games", Larry replied.

Larry outsmarted Sarah's lawyer. He kept talking after admitting that he ordered his bodyguard to 'take care' of Jason in hopes that it would be enough to clutter Ridley's brain and make him forget to ask what he meant by 'take care'. Rambling on like Larry did, asking Ridley so many questions, and to top it off, taunting Ridley to call Sarah to the stand again was enough to do the trick. And the whole case would have gone in Sarah's favour had Ridley asked what he meant. The SP Enterprises employees who lost their jobs, Mr. Ridley who was damaged by the loss of this case, and most importantly, Sarah, who felt like she lost her baby, who spent years planning and betraying some of her closest friends and her husband to become the most powerful woman in America. Their fates came down to Ridley forgetting to ask the most crucial question in this whole trial; "What did you mean when you told your bodyguard to take care of Jason?" If he had asked that, things would have ended differently.

"Is he really dead?" Beigler asked about Larry's bodyguard.

"Why do you ask?" Larry responded.

"C'mon Larry, I have seen you mourn a loss, and when you looked at his death certificate, I could tell you were faking it", Beigler explained.

"Do you know what ecdysis is?" Larry asked him.

"Extra what?" asked a confused Beigler.

"No, not extra dice; ecdysis, it's when snakes shed their skin. They do it every once in a while, it's something that they have to do to survive. The old worn out skin is replaced with newer skin, almost as though…the snake is reborn", Larry said as he smiled, suggesting that Snake may not have taken his last breath yet.

"Did you just know that he's still alive from looking at his death certificate?" Paul asked.

"His body was found on a park bench, and the time of death was around 8:30 pm." Larry answered.

"And? What's that supposed to signify?" Beigler curiously asked.

"Let's just say, it was a place that meant something for both of us." Larry did not want to explain thoroughly the significance of the location, but it was the same location and time that Snake interrogated Larry. It was that meeting in the park that got the two men closer.

"I'll be damned! So he faked his death to escape getting caught for killing the Brennan's?" Paul asked.

"No, because he still has one more hit I ordered him to do and I know he won't let me down."

"What?" Paul had a hunch as to whom Larry was referring to. "You still haven't gotten over that night?" Paul asked.

"That night? If I could go back in time to just one point, I would go back to that night and stop what happened. I lost everything I loved that night. David got what he deserved...but he wasn't alone!" Larry explained to the stunned Beigler. "Watch the news, she might commit suicide soon." There is still one more person that Larry needs to get retribution from; the second person that played a part in the death of his parents. The story never changed from the goal of 17 year old Larry Stone, beginning a mission to avenge his parent's death. He believed to have been successful when he killed David, but David's will shed light on what really happened, and Larry realized that his mission was not complete. Bidding his time in prison, thinking of a way to punish the second person involved in the crash, without harming his daughter. Larry's prayers were answered when his lawyer revealed that Sarah was not the owner. The rest of what happened after that was planned step by step, as Larry sat in his jail cell at night. And now, after almost 10 years, 17 year old Larry Stone is about to complete his retribution.

Sarah Phillips was a broken woman, all her hard work was gone and she had no idea how to pick herself up again. She cut all contact from the outside world, and she didn't even try to get her daughter back from Judy.

"Uncle Steve, could you do me a favor. Could you and Judy call Sarah and offer to keep Allie with you during the trial? And don't tell her I told you."

It's true that Judy was kind-hearted and that she wanted to babysit Allie during the trial. But it was Larry that called Steve to suggest that they take Allie.

"...Take care of her. But wait until the time is right...you will know when."

When Mark patted Larry on his head, that time when he visited him in prison for the last time. Larry looked up at Mark and whispered a new order for his confidant, and there were no details needed for Mark, he knew who Larry meant.

The game of chess never ended when Sarah overthrew Larry. Larry kept playing, and what he was doing this whole time was making sure to clear the chess board of every single piece. His daughter is out of harm's way, and the bodyguards are not there to protect Sarah anymore. The only thing left on the chess board was a lonely and vulnerable queen with no empire, and nothing to protect her from the ghost of Larry's dead knight.

"Sarah was right...You're a lying S.O.B! You planned this all along. This was never about Jennifer or Bonnie's retribution. It has always been about you...Its always been your retribution."

Paul Beigler, uttered those words to Larry after he revealed to him that Mark was still alive, and that he was ordered to kill Sarah. But Paul was right, the focus never shifted from Larry's goal of avenging his parent's death. And that goal was just half complete.

Sarah became distant and depressed, exactly how David felt after he lost everything. She had locked herself in her room for some time, much like what Larry did after losing his parents. But she felt it was time to get out of the house, She went out for a walk, she went to have coffee, and had no idea where to go or what to do next, so she decided to go back home again. She got back home and decided to take a shower. After getting out of the shower, she put her bathrobe on and she entered her dimly lit bedroom, without noticing the figure that was standing behind the door. The bathroom door was slammed shut, which made Sarah jump in fear and turn around. Even though the room was not appropriately lit, she still recognized the shadowy figure that was standing facing her. Her face became paler than the cotton white bathrobe that she had on, as if she had just seen a ghost. She didn't say anything because she felt that there was nothing left to say now; this was her end.

Sarah was frozen beside her bed, as the man slowly approached her, never taking his eyes off her while doing so, and when he was face to face with her, he pulled a gun that was tucked in the back of his pants. But it wasn't his usual silver gun; it was a desert eagle, the same desert eagle that belonged to Larry. It was in the hands of the police ever since Larry used it to kill David. But miraculously, the gun vanished from the police and was now in the hands of this man. The gun that belonged to Jack Stone was about to be used again to avenge his and his wife's death. The man raised the gun and pointed it at Sarah's temple, as he finally spoke.

"If there is one thing you should have learned from knowing Larry for so long, is that he is not a man to be messed with; because if you mess with Larry Stone, you are gonna get bitten by a snake!"

The End

EPILOGUE

It's the summer of 1975; Steve and Judy Nichols have just arrived at the adoption centre excited about the prospects of adopting their first child. Disappointment from the doctors' continued diagnosis that Judy is unable to bear a child didn't stop them from wanting to become parents. They were a loving couple, who have been married for five years, and who have dreamt of raising their own children. But since they couldn't bear their own, they started to look at other alternatives. The best option in Judy's eyes was adopting from an orphanage; the idea that she will take care of a child that is left alone, to give him shelter and a home that he desperately needs, was the best and only choice for her. Steve agreed and they contacted the local adoption agency to inquire about adopting a boy. They have plans in the future to adopt more kids but Steve wanted the first child to be a boy. The agency provided both domestic and international adoption which was a relatively new concept having just been introduced over a decade ago, and the couple looked at both options. One boy intrigued them; a 6 year old boy from Bulgaria, who had striking blue eyes and big bright smile. He lost both his parents to gang related violence, and he has been living in an orphanage since he was 3 years old, with no one coming forward to offer to adopt him. He speaks little English, which was impressive seeing as English was rarely spoken in his country. He loves to read and solve puzzles, which again was unique when compared to the other kids who just wanted to play with traditional toys. Steve and Judy were confident that this is the child for them, and they informed the agency about their decision.

The process to complete the adoption took well over two months, but when it was done, the child was ready to be flown to his new home. The joy was etched on his face during the nearly 13 hour flight for two reasons; he was excited he was finally going to be in a family and he was enjoying his first plane ride. After arriving in New York, the agency was there to welcome him and take him to his new parents who were waiting for him at the adoption centre. Wearing a red jumper and a small backpack on his back, the six year-old boy walked into the adoption center while holding the agents hand. The adoption agent pointed at Steve and Judy and whispered in the kids' ear that these are his new parents. As he saw them for the first time, his smile grew even bigger as he ran and hugged his new mother. Steve and Judy, now on their knees looking at their new son, were overjoyed.

"Hi, my name is Steve and this is Judy. What is your name?"

"...Marko"

www.ingramcontent.com/pod-product-compliance
Lightning Source LLC
Chambersburg PA
CBHW062136170626
46813CB00002B/719